TRAVELS WITH SUSHI
IN THE LAND OF THE MIND

Eduard Shyfrin

Illustrated by

Tomislav Tomic

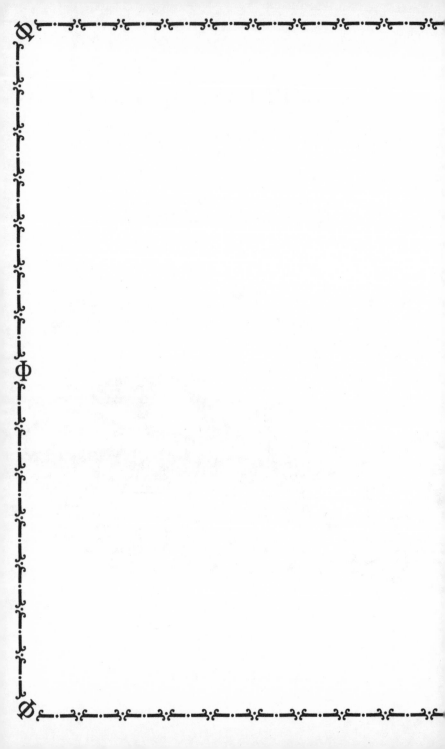

Contents

- Prologue -

'Time to get out now!' the children's grandmother called out, two brightly coloured beach towels held up in readiness.

Both Aaron and Stella pretended not to hear her over the crashing of the surf as they allowed the waves to sweep them in and out on the warm sand. They didn't look in her direction either, although from the corners of their eyes they could see that she was waving their towels at them while the rest of the family party was packing up behind her - folding chairs, rolling up mats and lowering the boldly striped umbrella.

'We're going for sushi,' their grandmother shouted, smiling as she watched them suddenly struggling to get to their feet in the rolling waters and running through the shallows towards her outstretched arms, hopping and exclaiming as the soles of their feet struck the occasional sharp pebble.

'Did you say sushi, Grandma?' Aaron panted as she wrapped him in his Avengers towel, rubbing himself vigorously against the chill of the light evening breeze.

'I had to get your attention somehow,' she laughed, cocooning his sister, Stella, in a second towel, which sported a picture of a young pop star.

'We are having sushi, though?' Stella asked, eyes wide with the suspicion that they'd been tricked into abandoning the fun of the ocean.

'Yes, my dear,' her grandmother laughed, towelling her hair. 'We all know how much you two love your sushi.'

The children hurriedly pulled on their shorts and T-shirts, not even bothering to put on their shoes as they ran after the rest of the family, who were wending their way to the small row of beachside restaurants. Every summer of their lives they had come to stay with their grandparents in the old family home by the great sea, with its weathered grey clapboarding and verandas, where their father had grown up with his siblings. Their evening trips to the ramshackle little sushi restaurant had become one of the many highlights of their holidays in what seemed to them to be the most beautiful spot in the north of the world.

For the rest of their lives, neither of them would ever be able to taste Japanese food without remembering the long, carefree days swimming from the beach and horse-riding in the mountains behind the town. On the rare days when the weather was wet, and on the long evenings in front of the fire, Aaron and his grandfather would play endless games of chess. It had become the boy's obsession, allowing him to show off his impressive maths skills - at the same time as exercising his highly active imagination. His favourite figure, the White Queen, represented in his mind all that was good, and all that should be protected and allowed to triumphin the world.

When they were finally persuaded to go to bed both children would then read beneath their bedclothes with torches, believing that their grandparents knew nothing about it. Of course they knew, as did their parents when they did the same thing on school nights at home, but nobody minded as long as Aaron and Stella both continued to excel in the classroom, and to exhibit the sense of fair-mindedness which marked them out as special amongst their peers. These qualities also made Stella the most popular girl in her year and the highest-performing pupil in the school.

'It is a rare thing,' her headmistress had told her proud parents, 'for a child to have such a well-developed set of principles at such a young age.'

There were only two waiters in the sushi restaurant, both of whom seemed to be on the premises every day throughout the summer season – Mr and Mrs Ekaku, a deeply courteous Japanese man and his tiny delicate wife. No matter how busy the restaurant became they never allowed their composure to be disturbed or their politeness to waver, and neither of them ever cracked a smile.

'Mr Aaron.' Mr Ekaku opened the door for them, bowing low to the children. 'And Miss Stella. Good to see you both again.'

The children returned the bow with equally solemn faces and then followed the adults to their usual corner table, the cushioned seats cool beneath the sun-burned backs of their legs.

'We have all worked up a good appetite on the beach,

Mr Ekaku,' their grandfather said, not bothering to look at the menus standing on the table. 'Will you bring us your usual selection? And plenty of them.'

Mr Ekaku bowed again. 'And the usual for you, Mr Aaron and Miss Stella?'

'Yes, please,' Aaron replied. 'Sixteen pieces of salmon sushi without wasabi.'

'And ten pieces of the same for me,' Stella said. 'And a Coke.'

'And a Coke for me too!' Aaron added quickly.

The grown-ups all laughed.

'Are you sure you wouldn't like to try some of the other varieties for once?' their grandmother asked. 'You might like them even better.'

'Quite sure, thank you,' the children replied in unison, as they always did whenever their grandmother asked the question. Neither of them wanted to risk trying something new, which might not taste quite as good as the sushi they knew and loved.

More people were coming in to the tables from the beach and others, more elegantly dressed, were arriving from the houses that lay behind the shops.

The noise levels started to rise as customers ate and drank and laughed. It was possible to see all the action in the steam-filled kitchens at the back as the chefs ran from place to place, while Mr and Mrs Ekaku moved calmly amongst the tables, making sure that everyone was served with whatever they wanted. As the sun set, the lights glowed warmly and the neatly clipped plants outside, which separated the restaurant from the beach, were lit from below by softly coloured bulbs.

The children ate faster than everyone else, concentrating on the food and paying little attention to the adult conversations going on around them. They could still feel the salt from the seawater tight on their skins and the sand in their hair and between their toes. Their growing muscles ached with a pleasant tiredness.

After an hour or so, the adults were asking one another if they wanted desserts or coffee or tea before paying the bill and going home to bed. As they tried to make up their minds, Mr Ekaku appeared from the kitchen holding a small silver tray on which sat two gold-coloured pieces of sushi. He bowed down to present the children with the tray, and the most delicious aroma either of them had ever experienced drifted up to their nostrils, filling their minds with warmth and tinting the busy scene around them with a kaleidoscope of different colours.

'Because you are two of our most regular customers,' Mr Ekaku said, 'and because you are experts in salmon sushi, our head chef would like to present you with his latest speciality. He would value your opinion.'

Even though their stomachs were full to bursting, the children picked up one piece of soft, warm sushi each, and the grown-ups asked for coffees and teas. When they placed the sushi on their tongues, a thousand different flavours seemed to burst from within the tiny golden parcels. The warmth spread over them like a thick woollen blanket as they sank back into their seats. The voices of their family and all the other diners merged together into one soothing sound, not unlike music or waves breaking on a shoreline, and the coloured lights on the plants seemed to dance before them before being engulfed by a descending darkness.

The children closed their eyes to bask in the sensations. When they opened them again, the restaurant had vanished.

– The Challenge –

Stella and Aaron found themselves standing in a cave amidst a small army of flickering candles, some as tall as the children themselves.

'Where are we?' Stella asked, her small voice echoing around the domed roof that stretched high above them, beyond the reach of the candlelight.

'Where are Granny and Grandpa?' Aaron asked, peering into the darkest corners of the cave – maybe his grandfather was hiding there, enjoying the joke of seeing them so baffled at the scene's sudden transformation.

'You are in the Mushi Land of the Mind,' a deep, musical voice announced. Echoes of the words rolled back and forth around the rocks, making it hard to tell where they came from.

The children spun round, their hearts beating fast, searching for the owner of this mellifluous voice. As their eyes adjusted to the gloom at the edges of the cave, they were able to make him out, standing a little above them on a rock. There was the scratch of a match and a lantern flared into life in the man's hand, casting flickering shadows up onto his face as it swung back and forth. He was probably overweight,

but it was impossible to see because he was wearing a billowing white caftan, elaborately embroidered with golden images of salmon sushi. On top of his long thick greying curls he wore a beret with the same motif embroidered on it. He opened his arms wide in a gesture of welcome, smiling kindly.

'My name is Salmon Mushi,' he said. 'And I am the leader of the Mushi tribe.'

'Why have you brought us here?' Aaron demanded bravely.

'And what have you done with Grandpa and Grandma and the rest of our family...?' Stella added, feeling a little tearful, but not wanting to show it.

'And Mr and Mrs Ekaku,' put in Aaron, his bottom lip trembling just a little.

'I have brought you here to tell you a story,' Salmon Mushi said. 'If you are wise, you will at least listen to what I have to say.'

Stella gripped her brother's hand tightly in case he was made to disappear like the others. Usually he would have pushed her away indignantly, but at that moment it was comforting to feel her touch.

'A story about what?' she asked, thinking that she

would rather be tucked up in bed with one of her grandparents reading her a story, but curious, just the same, to know what this strange, kindly man had to tell them.

'I want to tell you about the Supreme Ruler of All,' the man said. His melodic voice had a hypnotic effect on them as it bounced around the walls of the cave, reminding the children of sermons they had sat through in the house of prayer they attended with their parents, and the preachers they had seen on the television. Usually they found their minds wandering at such moments, but not this time.

'The Supreme Ruler of All?' Aaron repeated, enjoying the powerful sound of the title.

'The one who created our world and us, creatures with our own "self",' Salmon Mushi confirmed.

'Personally,' Aaron said, his courage rising, 'I'm not sure such a person even exists. I've never seen him.'

Salmon Mushi gave a little smile, showing a glint of white teeth in his thick beard, but did not bother to respond to Aaron's pronouncement. 'When the Supreme Ruler decided to create our world and us, he realised that nothing and no one could exist in his infinite presence, so as he created world after world, he hid more and more of himself. It was only once he was almost lost from view that our world emerged, together with us – beings with our own "self". But by making himself invisible he allowed evil to emerge because "self" without the Ruler is evil.'

Both children were squinting hard in their efforts to understand what Salmon Mushi was telling them, hoping that it would soon become clear how they had come to be in his presence at all.

'So, why doesn't he come back and do something about all this evil then?' Stella asked.

'If he's so supreme, he should be able to zap every bad guy in the world in an instant,' Aaron added, with not a little relish.

'In his kindness, the Supreme Ruler separated good from evil.' Again, Salmon Mushi continued as if they had not spoken. 'He appointed ten Great White Rulers to govern the Land of Mushi. The three highest Great White Rulers live high up in a castle on Memory Mountain; they are the Lords and Ladies of Will, Wisdom and Understanding. Down in the valley below are the other leaders: the Lords and Ladies of Love, Kindness, Self-Discipline, Beauty, Humility and Righteousness. With them also is the White Queen.

'The Supreme Ruler's plan was that his energy and information would be transmitted to the three main

leaders and from them to the leaders in the valley,
including the White Queen, and from there out into
the Mushi Land of the Mind, where, by the way, we
consume sushi and energy and information.'

Both Aaron and Stella were now so amazed by the
words that were swirling around the cave that they
had forgotten to be scared.

'So,' Aaron said, 'how does this Supreme Ruler pass
information down to everyone if no one can see him?'

'That is a very good question,' Salmon Mushi said.
'In our land we are all made up of information and
the Supreme Ruler, although invisible, supports
our existence at every moment. However, since his
concealment was so total that the Mushi could not
even sense his presence, he gave them a Book, in
which he told them about himself and set down some
rules for how to live.'

'Rules?' Stella asked suspiciously, not liking the sound
of that. Rules might interrupt her summer holiday,
making it more like school. 'What
sort of rules?'

'Instructions and
prohibitions, intended to
keep good and evil separate.'
Salmon Mushi explained.

'For instance, one of the most important prohibitions was that the Mushi were not allowed to eat rolls.'

'Seriously?' Aaron said. 'Rolls?'

'That's right.' Salmon Mushi nodded. 'As long as the Mushi obeyed all the Ruler's instructions and prohibitions, there was no evil in the Land of the Mind. The Mushi way of life was wonderful; there was no inequality, oppression or war. Every Musha was rewarded fairly for his or her work, and memory bits served as money.'

Stella raised her hand, as she might in class. 'Excuse me,' she said. 'What is a bit?'

'A bit is a unit of measurement of information. Since the storing of information requires a memory, that too is measured in bits. That is why memory bits serve as money in the land of the Mushi.'

'I'm sorry.' Stella shook her head, as if trying to shake the words into some sort of understandable order. 'How is it possible to measure information?'

Salmon Mushi gave a deep sigh and fell into silent thought for a moment, lifting his beret and running his fingers through his thick curls. The children waited with bated breath.

'I'll give you an example,' he said eventually. 'Imagine you have a coin with heads on both sides.'

Both children jumped with surprise as double-headed coins appeared in their palms.

'Now toss them in the air a few times.'

They did as they were told.

'They are always going to land heads-up, right?'

'Obviously, no matter how many coins you have with heads on both sides, you can never arrange them to convey any information, and your uncertainty is zero,' Aaron muttered under his breath, forcing his sister to stifle a giggle.

'If, however, you have a coin with a head on one side and tails on the other,' continued the Mushi, pausing long enough for them to realise that the coins in their hands now had different sides, 'then the number of states will equal two, which means that there is now some uncertainty. That is one "bit".'

Salmon Mushi closed his eyes for a moment and the children exchanged shrugs, neither of them sure that they quite understood what they were being told, but both still eager to hear more.

Then he continued. 'The Mushi chose leaders who they believed would judge people fairly and honestly, and once a year these leaders would gather for a feast at the castle of the White Queen. It was at one of these feasts that something happened that changed the lives of the Mushi in the Land of the Mind.' He paused for dramatic effect.

'What happened?' both children asked at once. Salmon Mushi smiled, pleased to see he had caught their attention.

'Forty years ago, the time came for the gathering of the Mushi leaders in the castle of the White Queen. They arrived on their phi-flyers...'

'Flying pies?' Stella giggled. 'That's silly!'

'Not the sort of pies you eat.' Salmon Mushi gave a small chuckle. 'It's spelled P-H-I, even though it sounds like "pie". They were phi-flyers, not flying pies.'
'But what are they?' Aaron insisted.

'OK.' Salmon Mushi took a deep breath, sitting down on the rock as if preparing himself for a long explanation. 'A long time ago the Supreme Ruler decided that he needed to cleanse the world which he had created...'

'Because of all the evil?' Stella said.

'Exactly!' The Musha nodded vigorously. 'So he sent a flood into the world, but decided to save one man and his family on the condition that they took with them a variety of birds and animals. We know from the Supreme Ruler's Book that he commanded this man to build a contraption, and told him the exact measurements that it should have. It had to be 50 cubits wide, 30 cubits high and 300 cubits long. If you divide 50 by 30 you get 1.66. Likewise, if you divide 50 plus 30 by 50 you get 1.6.'

The children exchanged puzzled looks. 'We don't get it,' Aaron said.

'Well, the great number of the Supreme Ruler is phi, which is equal to 1.618. We find this number everywhere in worlds created by him; in the construction of the galaxies of stars, atoms, the human body, art and architecture. That was why the contraption was called a phi-flyer. When they were inside it, the man and his family were completely safe from the flood, which drowned everyone and everything else.

'All the leaders of the Mushi had their own phi-flyers, and that is what carried them to this meeting at the White Queen's castle. Her servants had laid out a huge feast of a thousand different kinds of sushi, and they were all eating and drinking and talking when two phantoms appeared out of thin air, filling the room with intense feelings of excitement and anticipation, and the leaders with delicious sensations of well-being.'

'What, they just appeared in the air?' Aaron scoffed. 'From nowhere?'

'Life in the Land of the Mind follows quantum laws,' Salmon Mushi said, appearing faintly irritated at yet another interruption. 'I will explain that later. Let me finish this story first.'

'Sorry,' Aaron said.

'These two phantoms were the Lords of Flattery and Self-Justification, and the leaders were initially pleased to welcome two such pleasant fellows to the feast.

'"Oh, great rulers of Mushi," the Lord of Flattery began. "We are honoured to be in your company and to see you enjoying such a fine feast, but something is puzzling us."'

The children stifled giggles at the way Salmon Mushi used different voices for the different characters in his stories.

'"What would that be?" the leaders asked.
"Well," the Lord of Flattery beamed, "you give so much of your energy to leading this country with such wisdom, but you are not permitted to enjoy one of its greatest rewards. Have any of you ever tasted rolls?"
The leaders initially laughed at such a suggestion, explaining that they had been commanded by the Supreme Ruler never to eat rolls.

'"But they are so much tastier than sushi," the Lord of Self-Justification chipped in. "You have more than earned the right to experience this extra level of joy, even if you only try them once. Wise leaders need to have as many experiences as possible. Great thinkers need to satisfy their curiosity about everything, don't you think? Once you have tried them you will understand better why you have been banned from

eating them and you will then be able to ask the Supreme Ruler for forgiveness. I am sure a ruler as kind and wise as he is will understand why you need to grasp his rules from first-hand experience."

'The leaders, who were enjoying the company of these unexpected guests, started to debate their words, laughing and joking loudly as the door of the banqueting hall opened and several more phantoms floated in. These were wearing black hooded garments and carrying trays of rolls that filled the hall with aromas so tempting they made every atom of every leader's body yearn to touch them and savour the extraordinary flavours.'

The children were spellbound, remembering what had happened to them when they had been offered the special sushi and how it had smelled too good to resist; they hoped that Salmon Mushi was about to offer an explanation as to how it had led them to this cave.

'They all wanted to taste the rolls but they were nervous, wondering why the Supreme Ruler had commanded them not to. It wasn't long before the bravest – or perhaps the most foolhardy – volunteered to be the guinea pig.' The Musha closed his eyes as if relishing the sensations of the characters in his story. 'He raised a roll to his moist lips, parted them and placed the roll on his tongue. It melted immediately, releasing so many exquisite flavours that the leader couldn't stop himself from emitting the most unseemly groans of ecstasy. The others waited a few moments and then, when they saw that the taster had suffered no ill effects, they all reached out to take rolls for themselves.

'Once they had started, however, they could not stop. The wonderful flavours kept pulling them back for more. They closed their eyes to enjoy the sensations more intensely, giving out a chorus of groans and moans of pleasure. So engrossed did they become that none of them noticed the shadowy figures of the Wasabi Warriors, the army of the Black Queen, sneaking into the hall until it was too late. They were overwhelmed by the sheer numbers surrounding them as they ate, moaned in ecstasy and laughed hysterically at the table.'

'Didn't they try to resist?' Aaron asked. 'Didn't they fight back?'

'It was all over in minutes,' Salmon Mushi replied. 'They were seized, their memories were removed and they were sent to do hard labour in the Black Queen's energy plantations. Six of the Great Rulers were imprisoned inside an impenetrable shell and replaced by the Black Queen's governors – the Lords of Intolerance, Fear, Pride, Indifference, Betrayal and Despair. The White Queen's castle was besieged by the Wasabi warriors; information and energy ceased to

flow from the three highest Great Rulers. The White Queen and the six Great Rulers from the valley were cut off from the information energy, and instead it began to flow towards the Black Queen's leaders, slowly filling her reservoir.

'The Book that the Supreme Ruler had given to the Mushi was very dangerous to the Black Queen, so she took it from them and hid it in a cave on Memory Mountain.'

Salmon Mushi fell silent, allowing the full horror of the event to sink into the children's minds.

'So what has happened since then?' Stella asked eventually.

'Life in the Land of the Mind changed. Kings began to rule the Mushi; inequality and oppression entered their lives. Wars broke out over energy and information. The Mushi became divided into those in the east and those in the west. The leaders of one side declared that the Supreme Ruler wanted everyone to eat salmon sushi first, and then tuna sushi, while the leaders of the other side claimed the reverse was the only "true way". Religious wars broke out over matters as trivial as that.

'One tribe, which chose not to eat shrimp sushi, was almost wiped out by enemies. Fear and distrust grew everywhere. An investigation was launched, and dissatisfied Mushi, or any who dared to voice contrary opinions, had their memories removed and were exiled in the energy plantations of the Black Queen. Both the Western and the Eastern Mushi preached peace and kindness to one another, while both secretly working on developing neuron bombs capable of destroying the whole of the Land of the Mind.'

'That's crazy,' Stella said.

Salmon Mushi nodded his agreement. 'In forty days' time, the Black Queen's energy reservoir will be completely full and the White Queen's will have been drained dry. Then the Black Queen will have absolute and indivisible authority over the whole of the Land of the Mind.'

'Then what will happen?' Stella asked, exchanging worried looks with her brother.

'Then the Supreme Ruler will be obliged to destroy the Land of the Mind, and we will all perish.'

'I still don't understand why we have been brought here,' Aaron said, with a shiver. His feet were growing cold on the stone floor of the cave. 'What could we possibly do to help?'

'You can return the Supreme Ruler's Book to the people and destroy the power of the Black Queen.'

The children stared at each other for a moment, stunned. 'Why us?' Stella asked eventually.

'We know from the ancient books that children who eat particular amounts of salmon sushi without wasabi are the ones chosen to return the Book to the Mushi. Aaron, you always eat sixteen pieces and, Stella, you eat ten. Sixteen divided by ten is 1.6. And sixteen plus ten divided by sixteen is 1.62.'

'Phi!' both children exclaimed at once.

'Exactly. Very close to the Supreme Ruler's greatest number.'

'We are the result of a mathematical equation?' Aaron said, shaking his head in amazement.

'All the laws of nature, and everything in nature itself, is based on information, and information, in turn, is based on mathematics,' answered Salmon Mushi. He paused for a moment, as if lost in thought. Coming to, he held out two boxes and said, 'I need to give you something important.'

'What's in there?' the children asked, peering at the boxes.

'Open and see for yourselves,' replied Salmon Mushi as he placed a box in each of their hands.

Aaron and Stella opened their boxes, and were initially dazzled by a bright, multicoloured light. When their eyes grew accustomed to the glow, they each saw a bracelet of fine red string on which was attached a golden, shining phi.

'You must wear these at all times!' commanded Salmon Mushi.

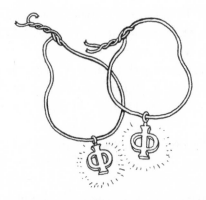

The children looked at him inquisitively and Salmon Mushi, sensing a question, continued, 'As I have told you before, phi is the number of the Supreme Ruler. It symbolises harmony, balance and beauty. These will serve to remind you that even in your darkest hour, the Supreme Ruler is always with you. It is prophesised by the ancient texts that one day a new generation will appear in our world – the Phi Generation. This generation will usher in a new era – an era of kindness, caring and compassion. For the prophecy to come to pass, the Book has to be returned to the people.'

But Stella was frowning. 'Why can't you do it yourselves?' she asked.

'We made a mistake,' Salmon Mushi said. 'Instead of fighting against the Black Queen, we went away from the world and into the Cave of Good.' He gestured around them. 'In his kindness, the Supreme Ruler provided us with an abundance of energy and sushi. We lost touch with what was happening elsewhere and now we are paying the price. We have been condemned to remain in the cave. We are helpless spectators as the Black Queen takes over the world.'

'Is there really no one among the Mushi who is brave enough to stand up to the Black Queen?' Aaron asked.

'A few have tried. In one of the countries of the Western Mushi, there was an army commander called Arthur. He was a great hero and the people loved him. One day the leader of that country ordered him to attack a neighbouring country.

'"But why would we do that?" he asked. "They are not planning to attack us."

'"But they have been enormously successful in their trading," his leader told him, "and have amassed huge reserves of memory bits. They are becoming stronger and stronger every day. We need to attack them now and take away their wealth before they are so powerful they will be able to wipe us out."

'Arthur was shocked and told the leader that he would not attack his fellow Mushi simply because they'd become rich. The leader was furious at this show of disobedience and ordered the secret police to seize him and put him in prison. Arthur heard about the plan in time; he gathered together his most loyal soldiers and led them into the darkest part of the forest, from where they could start their struggle of resistance.'

'Is there anyone else who would be prepared to fight?' Aaron asked.

'In the land of the Eastern Mushi there is a prince by the name of Salakh. He was born and brought up in a palace and wanted for nothing, but when he eventually rode out beyond the palace boundaries and saw how hard life was for ordinary Mushi and how much they suffered, he demanded that his leader did something about it. His leader, however, merely had him tried for treason, convicted and sentenced to death. His most loyal followers helped him break out of jail and they all now dwell in the desert, awaiting their opportunity to stage an uprising.'

'So what exactly do you want us to do?' Stella asked.

'The first thing you must do is climb Memory Mountain, open up the cave in which the Book is kept and return it to the Mushi. You will not be alone; the Supreme Ruler will be with you. The doors to the cave are both open and closed at the same time. If you are worthy, the Supreme Ruler will open them for you; but you need to understand that the Land of the Mind operates by different rules to the world in which you have lived so far – it follows quantum laws.'

'Which means?' Aaron asked.

'In a quantum world, a particle is in a superposition of states until it is measured, as if it is spread in space, and only after it is measured does it take the physical form that is familiar to us – like a small tennis ball. The same is true of the Black Queen. No one has ever seen her, but she exists everywhere at the same time. You can only deal with her by measuring her, but not everyone is capable of doing this. In the quantum world, you cannot measure both energy and time with absolute precision. The more you know about one, the less you know about the other. This is why, from out of nothing, pairs of particles may appear. This is the case with the Lords of Flattery and Self-Justification – they appear and disappear out of nothing.

'In the world you live in, there are four dimensions: length, height, width and time. In the Land of the Mind, however, there are also the infinite dimensions of good and evil. Until you do something bad, you are in the dimension of good, and the Wasabi Warriors have no power over you. If you do just one evil deed, however, you immediately fall into the dimension of evil, and they will then have full power over you. Servants of the Black Queen can appear and disappear at will. Connections exist in the mental space between the Mushi.'

Both children shook their heads, confused, and Salmon Mushi let out a small sigh of frustration. Then he pulled himself together to think of a better way to explain the concept of quantum law.

'We are mentally connected to those we love,' he said, 'as well as to our friends and acquaintances, and even some objects. These connections can vary in power and levels of activity, but an evil act will always result in an explosion and the destruction of positive mental connections.'

It was all very hard to take in. Aaron thought that maybe they'd do best to focus on practical details – maybe he'd be able to master those, at least. 'So how do we get to this mountain?' he asked.

'You must pass through the zones of the Black Queen's leaders, and defeat them. Then you must climb Memory Mountain and open the doors to the cave where the Book is kept. You will travel in a phi-flyer, which will be given to you by the Supreme Ruler. While inside it you will be completely protected. It will appear and disappear and move only according to the will of the Supreme Ruler.

'Before you arrive in each of these leaders' countries, the phi-flyer will give you the weapons and the tools you will need to be victorious. The wise raven, Sophie, will always be at your side. She represents the three main Great White Leaders who live on the Memory Mountain, and will advise you in any difficult situations you encounter.'

'A wise raven?'
Aaron rolled his eyes.

'Sophie the raven can be both a particle and a wave, whichever she decides at the time. She can also appear and disappear at any point in mental space.'

'How can something be a particle and a wave at the same time?' Aaron's head was beginning to ache from the effort of concentration.

'That is another characteristic of a quantum world. I'll give you an example. If you take a plate with two slots, place a screen behind it and fire an electron in the direction of the slots, what do you think will happen?'

'The electron will probably pass through one of the slots,' Stella answered for her brother.

'That would seem logical,' Salmon Mushi agreed. 'And then you might expect that an imprint of the electron, like that of the tennis ball, will appear on the screen behind the slot. But in fact that is not what will happen. A series of dark and light stripes will form on the screen behind the slot.'

'And what does that mean?' Aaron asked.

'It means that the electron behaves like a wave and will pass through both slots at the same time.'

'That's impossible!' the children said at once.

'It may be unimaginable to you, but it is a fact. And that is not all. If measuring devices are placed near each slot, the behaviour of the electron will change. In that case, it will behave like a tennis ball and pass through one slot or the other.'

'But why does that happen?' Aaron asked.

Salmon Mushi smiled and shrugged. 'There are many possible explanations, but no one knows the precise reason.'

There was a pause as the children took this in.

Then something else occurred to Stella. 'Why a raven?' she asked.

'You remember the first phi-flyer that I told you about, and the man who survived the flood with a variety of animals?' asked Salmon Mushi.

They nodded.

'Well, when the floodwaters dropped, he let out a raven, because ravens are highly intelligent. Its task was to return to tell the man what had happened to the world while they were in the phi-flyer. That raven was called Sophie.'

'You will also have a guide – my nephew – to steer you along the right path. He is called Cassie.'

Salmon Mushi signalled to someone behind them and a young man stepped out of the shadows, lighting a lamp as he came. He was dressed in the same way as his uncle, but his caftan fell gracefully around his tall, slim body and his face had the radiant glow of youthful strength. His bearing suggested he was a trained warrior, but his eyes were gentle and kind, and his smile totally dazzling. Stella let out a dreamy sigh before catching her brother's mocking eye.

'The cave on Memory Mountain is surrounded by zones of oblivion,' Salmon Mushi warned. 'Cassie

knows the safe passages.
The Black Holes of Glory,
Wealth and Power lie in
wait along the way; be
careful not to fall into
their clutches.'

'What is a Black
Hole?' Stella asked.

'It is a body that
possesses a huge
force of gravitational
attraction and, when
a certain boundary,
called an event horizon,
is crossed, nothing and
no one can escape.'

Salmon Mushi waved again
and two servants appeared from
the shadows carrying devices with screens showing
green stripes. 'These are your energy counters. When
a red line appears on the screen it means that your
energy level is too low. Although the Supreme Ruler
will always be with you, you may appeal to him three
times. It's up to you to decide when.'

'Why can't we just appeal to the Supreme Ruler now,'
Aaron asked, 'and get him to sort everything out?'

'The Supreme Ruler only ever intervenes when he sees that people have already done the maximum that they can do. He gave us our minds and bodies for a reason and wants us to use them. And finally...'

He held two boxes out to them, gesturing for them to open them. Inside they found red buttons. 'If you feel you no longer have the strength to continue with the mission, you can press these red buttons and the Supreme Ruler will send you back to your world. You can even press them now if you want to...'

Silence fell as Aaron and Stella stared at one another, both trying to work out if the other wanted to accept the mission or return to the safety of their known world. In the silence they heard a flapping sound close to their ears. The breeze from the wings of Sophie, the wise raven, ruffled their hair. It made the flames of the candles sputter as she appeared from above and settled on the floor between them.

'You can choose to go back,' she croaked. 'Of course you can, and tell yourselves that millions of people live normal, peaceful lives without having to make any effort to overcome any of the great evils in the world. But bear in mind that you may never again be offered an opportunity like this. It is a great honour to be able to provide a direct service to the Supreme Ruler.'

'We accept the mission!' they cried in unison, snapping shut the lids of the boxes.

- The Land of Intolerance -

Cassie stepped forward into the light and bowed to them respectfully. Stella and Aaron were both in awe.

'It's an honour to meet you,' Cassie said, appearing not to notice their embarrassment. 'I will be accompanying you on your journey. Please, this way.'

The bobbing light from his lantern revealed a corridor which neither of them had noticed before. They walked for several hundred metres away from the cave, both being careful not to stub their toes on the corners of the rocks, before reaching a large iron door covered in beautiful entwined symbols – clearly the work of a highly skilled blacksmith. They could sense Sophie the raven swooping from ledge to ledge in the shadows above their heads, stirring the otherwise still air with her wings.

The door opened silently as it sensed their approach, with none of the creaking of ancient hinges or scraping along the ground that they might have expected, revealing another identical door ahead. The first door glided shut behind them and a few seconds later the second door opened equally smoothly to reveal what looked at first like another cavern. But this one was so filled with dazzling light it took a few seconds for their eyes to readjust to the glare. Cassie extinguished his lamp and waited patiently for them to take in their surroundings.

'This is the Supreme Ruler's phi-flyer,' he announced as the raven swooped past them and settled on a perch, fussily shaking herself free of some dust that had attached to her feathers in the corridor.

Before them were three lavishly cushioned leather chairs, two in front and one behind. A large screen flickered across from them. Along the sides of the room were tables laden with piles of sushi, in a hundred different colours they had never seen before, glistening like succulent jewels. Behind the chairs stood a large machine, which was emitting a low hum. They guessed this was one of the energy sources that Salmon Mushi had talked about.

'Please,' a voice addressed them from every direction, 'make yourselves comfortable.'

Cassie gestured for them to take the two front seats before sitting in the one behind them. The screen flashed into life and a map appeared.

'This is the journey you will be going on,' the voice intoned, as a red arrow appeared at the bottom of the map next to the words 'The Cave of Good'. It pulsated for a moment and then moved, leaving a trail of red dots as it went, up the map to the top, where they could read the words, 'Memory Mountain'. Along the way, the red dotted line passed through all the territories of the Black Queen's leaders: Intolerance, Fear, Pride, Indifference, Betrayal and Despair. The hum from the energy source throbbed louder and the children realised that the phi-flyer had set off without them feeling a thing. They settled back into the softness of the chairs and prepared their minds for whatever adventures lay ahead. An exhilarating mix of excitement and nerves made their hearts beat and their blood run faster.

At exactly that moment, six of the Black Queen's leaders were sitting in a hall the size of a cathedral inside her castle. All of them were shrouded in thick robes to protect them from the damp chill oozing from the stone walls, their hoods pulled up to cover their heads and shadow their faces. Only the fog of their breath was visible as it met the cold air and condensed into vapour. At the end of the hall stood an enormous energy tank, on the side of which was a counter with numbers flashing on the display.

'My loyal leaders.' The Black Queen's voice came from every direction, echoing around the pillars and up into the vaulted roof spaces. 'In just forty days, our energy

Travels With Sushi in the Land of the Mind

reservoir will be completely full and we will have absolute control over the Land of the Mind. None of you have ever seen me because I am everywhere, but once the reservoir is full I will finally stand before you in a form you can comprehend.'

She laughed, the sound howling around them like a bitter winter wind, making some of them pull their robes a little tighter. All the leaders joined in with the laughter, creating a sound so cold and so terrible that its effect chilled places that were far beyond earshot.

Both Aaron and Stella shivered in their warm phi-flyer seats, without knowing what had sent the ripple of ice running through their blood. The moment passed and they forgot about it as the phi-flyer's engines quietened and then came to a stop. A message appeared on the screen.

'Zone of Intolerance. Weapon: Zeno gun.' An image of a rifle appeared.

'What is a Zeno gun?' Aaron asked the raven. Sophie stretched her wings wide and shook her feathers out, taking her time before replying as if he had woken her from a nap. She seemed to enjoy being the one with all the answers and making them wait to hear them. 'Have you forgotten already that you are in the Land of the Mind?' she squawked eventually, 'and that the Land is subject to quantum laws?'

'That still doesn't explain what a Zeno gun is,' Stella said, a little annoyed.

'Well, if the quantum system is constantly measured, then nothing will happen in it,' the raven continued, 'and it will be as if it's frozen in time. The Zeno gun works on the same principles. If it is directed at someone, they will freeze and be unable to act in any way, giving you an advantage over them.'

'That is so cool,' Aaron murmured as they made their way towards the exit. He saw the gun lying next to the door. 'I'll take it,' he said, before his sister or Cassie could pick it up.

'You're welcome,' Stella sniffed. 'I hate guns.'

Aaron didn't respond. The weapon felt reassuringly solid in his hands, and he secretly hoped he was going to get a chance to try it out soon.

As the doors of the phi-flyer opened, they stepped out into a sun-drenched valley. There were meadows to either side, filled with wild flowers and neatly divided by a narrow road that stretched ahead of them, snaking up into the mountains.

'Follow me,' Cassie said, setting off down the road without looking back.

The children struggled to keep up with his long strides. Every so often, one of them would step on a stone with their thin shoes and let out a squeak of pain, but Cassie never looked round and never slowed his pace. It seemed that the mission they were on was more important than any passing discomforts. The sun was hot, and the gun began to weigh uncomfortably in Aaron's arms. He envied the raven as she soared effortlessly above them, enjoying the thermal currents flowing down from the mountains, which lifted her higher and higher.

After several hours' walking, they reached the edge of a gorge. Cassie finally stopped and turned, apparently unaffected by the long, strenuous hike.

'I cannot go any further with you,' he told them, with an apologetic smile. 'We Mushi from the Cave of Good must not mingle with the other Mushi. But this road will lead you to your destination, and it will also lead you back out again. I will wait for you. Good luck.'

He shook their hands, then sat down on the grass at the side of the road, lay back amongst the flowers, stretched his arms above his head and apparently fell instantly asleep in the sun. Aaron and Stella exchanged looks, neither sure what to say and both feeling nervous at the thought of continuing into the unknown without the comfort of Cassie's protection. The raven had risen so high in the sky that she had become little more than a black speck as she circled aimlessly around, waiting for the journey to continue. Aaron gave his sister a curt nod. The two of them mustered their strength and continued along the road in silence, with no idea of what dangers might be lying in store around every corner. After walking for several more hours, every part of them aching with tiredness, they found themselves entering a town. They looked for someone to ask for food or water, but the streets were strangely deserted. Then, they heard an angry rumble in the distance.

'What's that noise?' Stella asked.

'Sounds like a crowd,' Aaron replied. 'They sound excited about something.'

'No, not that. Something else. Listen.'

They stood still for a moment.

'It sounds like someone crying,' said Stella.

Aaron could hear it now, too: a low sobbing noise of such complete despair that it tore painfully at their own hearts, even though neither of them was feeling remotely sad. They followed it round several corners, eventually coming upon a man curled up in a tight ball against the corner of a house, as if trying to make himself as small and invisible as possible. He jumped when Stella knelt down and put her hand on his shoulder; he hadn't heard them coming over the sound of his own sobs, and hadn't seen them because his eyes were squeezed shut, as though to lock out the entire world and all its horrors.

The children squatted down beside him and Stella stroked his arm. Eventually his weeping subsided, and he was able to find enough breath to speak.

'What is the matter?' Stella asked. 'Why are you so sad?'

'Yesterday, in the market,' he said, gulping for air, 'my wife got into an argument with another woman and said that she didn't believe that the Supreme Ruler cared about the order in which the Mushi eat sushi, and that he will judge them according to their deeds, not their eating habits. A stallholder overheard and reported my wife to the authorities. She was arrested and thrown into a dungeon. All our property was confiscated, including our house, and today she is due to be executed.'

The children gasped and looked at each other in horror. How awful!

'What is your name?' Aaron asked.

'Guido. My name is Guido the Carpenter, and my wife is Marie.'

'Where is the execution taking place?'

'In the main square, in a few minutes.'

'Is that what all the noise is about?' Stella asked.

'Yes. Everyone has to watch. It is the law. The authorities believe that people need to be shown what will happen if they stray from the rules. Disobedience of any sort cannot be tolerated.'

'We have to do something!' Stella said, and Aaron nodded his agreement.

'What can two children do against the whole Mushi army?' Guido asked.

'Even when a sword is being held above a person's head,' the raven cackled from the roof where she had landed above them, making them jump, 'they should not despair, but should continue to believe that the Supreme Ruler will save them – if that is what is meant to be.'

'Come on.' Aaron helped Guido to his feet. 'Take us to the main square. We need to hurry.'

They ran through the deserted backstreets as the noise of the crowd grew closer and increasingly excited, eventually emerging into a large square where all the people of the town were packed tightly around a stage, jostling for a good view.

As the children pushed their way through the closely pressed bodies, they heard the sound of trumpets and the banging of drums; soldiers dragged a woman up onto the platform. She was in a sorry state, covered in dirt and bruises, her clothes ripped by the cruel and careless hands of her jailers. They pushed her down roughly into a chair, which had a high back with a hood-like attachment. A self-important Mushi, dressed in a black coat with an expression to match, climbed up and stood beside her. He unrolled a scroll and read loudly and slowly to the people below, as if savouring every moment of the condemned woman's agony. Clearly, he enjoyed being the centre of attention and being able to exert authority over so many people.

'In the name of the Great Ruler of Intolerance and the Eight Mushi, it has been decreed that this woman, by the name of Marie, has dared to state publicly that the Supreme Ruler does not care in which order the Mushi eat sushi.' He rolled the rhyming words around his tongue dramatically. 'By uttering such heresy, she has blasphemed against the Supreme Ruler. Moreover, she has confessed to being a secret agent of the Mushi tribe who do not eat shrimp sushi.'

'She must have been tortured to have confessed to such a crime,' Guido whispered to Aaron. 'She is just an ordinary wife and mother. She is not a spy for anyone. It is ridiculous. My poor Marie, what terrible things must they have done to make her admit to such things?'

'As a result of her actions,' the man continued from the platform, 'the woman by the name of Marie is sentenced to permanent loss of memory and permanent exile to the energy plantations of our beloved Black Queen. All her property, including her family members, will be passed to the loyal patriot who reported her crimes.'

A sound went up from the crowd that could have been cheering, but also sounded like it might be jeering, depending on what you hoped to hear. The man in black, who was now rolling up his scroll as if it were some rare and valuable artefact, looked around uneasily for a moment, then relaxed as an enormous executioner, his deeply scarred face partly shadowed by a red hood, stepped out onto the platform beside him.

The executioner glowered threateningly down at the crowd, many of whom drew back in fear. He made a grand show of walking to the chair and lowering the hood over Marie's head, which was jerking from side to side in helpless, wide-eyed panic. Some people gasped in horror, clamping their hands across their mouths, their eyes as wide as the victim's. Others squeezed their eyes tightly shut, as if by not seeing it, they could make the horror cease to exist. The sounds of the cheering continued, mainly from the throats of Mushi soldiers and from those close enough to them to be intimidated into joining in.

'That's the memory extraction hood,' Guido gasped. 'We're too late.'

'Stop!' A girl's voice rang out over the noise, and everyone looked around to see who had dared to speak up so forcefully.

'It's Stella!' Aaron exclaimed, jumping up and down to see over the people's heads as his sister clambered up onto the platform and pushed the shocked executioner back from the chair. Taken by surprise, the huge man stumbled off balance. He raised an angry fist and then lowered it again. Even a man as callous and cruel as he hesitated to hit a young girl in front of a crowd.

'Leave her alone!' Stella shouted, her whole body trembling with righteous anger. 'She hasn't done anything wrong. She just voiced an opinion.'

'Treason!' screamed the black-clad Mushi official. 'This is another agent of the Mushi tribe who do not eat shrimp. Seize her!'

Mushi soldiers armed with neuron pistols were forcing their way through the crowd, punching and kicking people out of their way.

Sophie the raven swooped low over Aaron's head. 'Do something, boy!' she shrieked as she circled above him, furiously flapping her wings. 'Use your weapon.'

Startled back into action by the bird's cry, Aaron ducked down, forcing his way through the crowd at waist height with Guido close behind him. By the time they emerged at the bottom of the platform steps, the soldiers were already surrounding Stella, who had placed herself between Marie and her persecutors. Aaron raised the gun to his shoulder, took aim and fired. The soldiers froze.

'Get Stella and Marie!' he shouted to Guido. 'And then run. I'll cover you.'

Guido leapt onto the stage and grabbed Marie and Stella by the hand, dragging them down the steps and into the nearest side alley. Aaron caught up with them, aware of the soldiers' boots getting closer behind them as they unfroze and gave chase. 'We need to find the road back to the phi-flyer!' he shouted. 'It's just the other side of the gorge.'

'We can't run any more,' Guido wheezed, and Aaron could see that both he and his wife were close to collapse.

'Keep going,' Aaron urged. 'You can do it.'

As they came around the next corner, however, their path was completely blocked.

'A landslide,' Guido groaned. 'We're doomed.'

The thunder of the soldiers' boots and the rattling of their weapons were growing louder behind them.

'I'll hold them back with the Zeno gun!' Aaron shouted. 'You find a way through.'

As the other three started pulling at the rocks, throwing them frantically to each side, Aaron raised his gun and waited the few seconds it took for the first detachment of soldiers to appear around the corner with their pistols drawn and ready. Just as they started to fire he squeezed the trigger and they froze, blocking the path of those running up behind them. Glancing down at the gun, Aaron noticed a red line, indicating that its power level was running low. How could it have lost power so quickly? He had expected it to be a more effective weapon than that.

'Faster!' he shouted to the others, running to help them as they desperately scrabbled forward through the rocks. The green line on the gun flickered one more time and turned to red as other soldiers managed to push their way through their frozen comrades. A gap had appeared between the stones, just big enough for them to wriggle through one at a time. Aaron swung back and pointed the gun at the advancing soldiers, hoping they couldn't see the red light. But they didn't stop.

A low rumble shook the ground beneath them, and the soldiers lowered their guns, looking around to see if it was another landslide; but no rocks were falling from anywhere. Aaron watched in astonishment as the ground between him and soldiers erupted with a roar so loud it must have been heard for hundreds of miles. Rocks and stones hurtled up out of the ground like a volcano, then rose in the air and clattered back to the earth to form a mighty wall in front of the shocked soldiers. Seizing the opportunity, Aaron followed the others, wriggling through the gap to emerge into the calm, sunny fields beyond.

'Come on!' he shouted. 'Back to the phi-flyer!'

Guido and Marie were too exhausted to run, but Aaron managed to cajole them slowly forward for several hours. They rounded the last bend and found Cassie still stretched out amongst the soft meadow flowers. He sat up as he heard them approach, looking thoroughly refreshed from his rest. Marie and Guido collapsed, exhausted, onto the grass beside him.

'Who are they?' Cassie asked.

'These two have saved our lives,' Marie murmured through dry, cracked lips. 'But I don't know what we will do now. We have lost everything and they will certainly kill us if we ever try to go back.'

Sophie landed on the grass between them and folded her wings. 'Anyone who has left the Zone of Evil must never return there,' she squawked.

'Come with us,' Stella suggested. 'We need trustworthy friends.'

Guido cradled his wife in his arms. 'We would be honoured to be your friends,' he said. 'But we will never be able to repay you for what you have done for us today.'

They all helped to lift Marie and carry her into the phi-flyer, where there were now five comfortable seats waiting for them.

Meanwhile in the castle of the Black Queen, five of her leaders were still sitting in the cold, grand hall, anxiously watching the stream of numbers flowing into the energy tank, which seemed to be slowing down.

At the same time, the White Queen was in her own castle, sitting on an intricately carved throne set with a thousand pearls. Her long, thick blonde hair was swept up to frame her perfectly symmetrical, tranquil face. It was impossible to see the doubts and fears that raged inside her beneath the composed exterior. On the warm golden stone of the walls around her, six portals buzzed and crackled with static, making it impossible for her to communicate with her leaders. In front of her stood one of her commanders, the Lord of Bravery.

'Your Majesty,' he announced, 'the castle is totally surrounded by an army of Wasabi warriors. There is no way in and no way out.'

'So we are besieged?' the Queen asked. 'Is there any hope for us?'

'The walls are high and strong,' said the Lord of Bravery, seeking to comfort her. 'They cannot be penetrated. We have wired them so that the magnetic field will block the electrical impulses of neurons and cannons.'

'But that will use a lot of energy,' the Queen pointed out. 'And our supplies are running low.'

The Lord of Bravery glanced at the crackling screens and then the energy tank standing in the corner of the room. Only a thin green line remained on the display. 'We must not despair, Your Majesty. Our friends at the Cave of Good tell me that two strangers, who were written about and predicted in the ancient texts, have arrived in our land. They have come to fight the Black Queen's leaders, one of whom has already suffered a defeat. The transfer of energy to the Black Queen's reserves has been reduced, while ours has started to increase a little. I hear also that both Arthur and Salakh are raising armies in the forest and in the desert, and will soon have sufficient numbers to mount effective attacks. We must continue to put our trust in the wisdom of the Supreme Ruler, to whom, Your Majesty, your connection never falters.'

'Of course.' The Queen spoke slowly, as if choosing her words carefully. 'And of course none of us can know what his ultimate plans might be. So until he chooses to reveal them to us, we must continue the struggle to control our own fate.'

- The Land of Fear -

Aaron, Stella and their two new friends fell into an exhausted sleep as the phi-flyer purred into action. When they opened their eyes they had no idea how much time had passed or how far they had travelled, but they felt refreshed and sensed that they had reached their next destination.

There was a new message waiting for them on the screen: 'Attention. Zone of Fear. Weapons: staff, Zeno gun, torch and sling.'

'Why would we need a staff?' Aaron wondered out loud.

Sophie the raven strutted across the floor below the screen, fixing them with a beady black eye like a small feathered professor delivering a lecture. 'The ruler of the Zone of Fear knows all your fears. He knows that you are afraid of heights, Aaron, and that you, Stella, are terrified of spiders. He will be planning to exploit that information to the full. The staff will help you to overcome your fears.'

'How?' Stella asked, shuddering at the mention of spiders, and remembering how often her brother had used her phobia to tease her and make her run off squealing.

'It is the staff of the Supreme Ruler. The wise man says, "If I pass through the gorge of the shadow of death, I will not fear, as your staff is with me." So, now it is time for us to go.'

Aaron armed himself with the recharged Zeno gun and the staff, while Stella picked up the torch and the sling. Cassie opened the door for them.

'It's OK,' he said with a reassuring smile, seeing them hesitate. 'Don't be afraid.'

Aaron and Stella led the way through the door and Guido and Marie followed behind, struggling to disguise their own fears but willing to follow their two saviours wherever they might go. Cassie walked quietly in the rear, which helped boost their confidence.

It was twilight as they emerged from the phi-flyer, and they found themselves deep in a forest with trees stretching away from them in every direction. They had not gone more than a few paces when Stella felt the brush of a cobweb against her face. She screamed as a long, thin leg, covered in fine, spiky hairs, entwined itself almost lovingly around hers.

Jumping backwards, tearing at it desperately, she stumbled into Marie's arms. 'It's a spider!' she cried, gasping for air. 'A giant one! I felt its leg against mine. It was huge!'

'Shh.' Marie held her tightly and stroked her head. 'I don't mind spiders. I'll protect you.' She turned to Aaron. 'Give her the staff,' she instructed. 'I'll lead the way.'

Aaron passed the staff over, and as Stella gripped the shaft a light glowed all around it, revealing webs stretching out on both sides of the path. All of them were filled with huge spiders, now roused from their slumbers and apparently curious as to what prey might have wandered within their reach. Their eyes burned with reflections of the staff's light, and they reached out to try to grab the passers-by and pull them into their sticky webs, emitting hissing noises as they moved that chilled the blood of all who heard them. Stella found that as the warm glow from the staff seeped into her, she was able to breathe more easily. She lost the urge to scream and the creatures shrank back from the light when she thrust it at them. She watched with something close to amusement as they curled their legs up into their bodies, suddenly appearing small and harmless, and wondered how she could ever have believed they could harm her.

After several hours' walking, they emerged from the forest in the dead of night and found themselves on the edge of a precipice, staring out into a blackness that not even the glow of the staff could illuminate. The path along the side of the cliff face was no wider than one of Aaron's narrow feet. On one side was rock and on the other, the unknown. He picked up a stone and threw it into the darkness. They all waited in silence to hear it land. The distant sound reached them several seconds later.

'This is too high,' Aaron said, pressing his back against the rocks, every muscle in his body trembling with fear, every nerve end stripped raw. He couldn't take a step in any direction. 'I won't be able to balance. I'll fall and be killed. You go on without me.'

'Don't be ridiculous,' Stella scolded him. 'Take the staff.'

Aaron gripped it tightly like a lifeline, and immediately felt calmness settle over him as it lit up the path ahead. They moved slowly forward until they reached a rope bridge stretching over the deep, black gulf below. The bridge swung sickeningly back and forth beneath their feet as they trusted their weight to its slender ropes, but still Aaron was able to keep the feelings of panic under control.

The crossing seemed to go on forever. As they wobbled their way over, inch by swaying inch, dawn broke through the surrounding mountains and they were able to see just how deep the gorge was. Trees that would have looked like giants from the ground resembled the scenery from a child's toy farm when seen from the bridge swinging high above. Sophie swooped and dived around them as they concentrated on keeping their balance, clearly enjoying the morning breezes. She settled way out of sight in the trees below for a while before reappearing and soaring up above them once more.

By the time they had reached the safety of solid ground on the other side, fresh morning sunlight bathed the oasis that lay before them in a golden, glowing light. All around them exotic flowers were opening up after their night's slumbers, stretching their brightly coloured petals and yawning at the start of another day in paradise, awaiting the arrival of hummingbirds and honey bees to spread their pollen.

Beneath the palm trees the travellers found tables set up for them with plates of delicate sushi and drinks as colourful as the surrounding blossoms and birds. They all felt safe and free from fear. After eating and drinking they lay down and slept for a few hours in the long, soft grass, restoring their strength before continuing their journey.

'This is where I must leave you again,' Cassie told them when they were all awake. 'You go on without me and I will catch up with you soon. Remember, you have nothing to fear except fear itself.'

'He just wants to spend more time eating and sleeping,' Aaron muttered to his sister.

'Oh, shut up,' Stella said, jabbing him playfully in the ribs.

'Follow the path,' Cassie told them. He didn't seem to have heard Aaron's grumbling. 'And I will see you again soon.'

Refreshed, and feeling all pumped up after conquering their fears, the four of them strolled on through the luscious wild gardens, laughing and wondering what adventures might now lie ahead of them.

After several hours, they came upon a small town built of white bricks that shone brightly in the hot sun. A crowd of people were standing around a building that looked like a school, but there were no sounds of children's voices. In fact, the building seemed shrouded in silence. The crowd were all talking at once; some of them were crying and clinging onto one another as if to stop themselves from collapsing. A tall, fair-haired woman was moving among them, consoling those who were most distressed and giving instructions to others; she wore a dusty white gown that looked as if it might once have been elaborately embroidered but was now worn thin with use and bleached by the sun. She spotted the new arrivals and walked over.

'Greetings, strangers,' she said, and they were struck by the strength and beauty of her face with its high cheekbones, slender arched nose and skin stained the colour of olives by the sun. 'I am Erika, the leader of the Mushi tribe who do not eat shrimp sushi.'

Aaron stepped forward. 'My name is Aaron,' he said, surprised by how firmly Erika gripped his hand. 'And this is my sister.'

'Stella,' his sister added.

'What's happening here?' Aaron asked.

'We have a terrible problem,' she said. 'A fanatical Eastern Mushi, wearing enough explosives to kill us all, has taken over this school building where our children were resting in the shade after a long night's walk. He is threatening to kill them all if he doesn't get what he wants.'

'What does he want?' Stella asked.

'He wants us to change the way we worship the Supreme Ruler, but we have no way of doing that. He doesn't believe us. We have no idea what to say to him that will persuade him to spare our children's lives.'

Aaron was aware of the weight of the Zeno gun in his hands. He suddenly felt that the responsibility for this situation was resting on his shoulders. He remembered the courage that Stella had shown by stepping up onto the platform with Marie and challenging the executioner and soldiers, and how it had felt to walk along the bridge once his fear had been vanquished. He looked around at the crowd. It seemed obvious what had to be done. There were plenty of people, more than enough to rush in and rescue the children – if he could just get into the building and shoot the Eastern Mushi with the Zeno gun.

'I'll help you,' he said. 'Be ready to come in and grab the children when you hear me shout.'

He strode through the crowd towards the building before his sister or the others had time to protest at the foolishness of charging in without knowing what might be awaiting him. As the crowd realised what was happening, they fell silent. All eyes turned to the building and the boy walking towards it, everyone preparing themselves for the explosion that would end everything.

The closer he got to the door, the more Aaron's body shook with fear and adrenalin. It felt like his limbs were moving in slow motion, like he was pushing against a great force. By the time he had reached the door it was nearly impossible to move. Almost paralysed with fear, he turned back to see a hundred pairs of eyes willing him on, pleading with him to find the necessary courage. He understood that if he didn't overcome his fear now, he would be a slave to the Lord of Fear forever, and the mission would have failed. After a few motionless moments he turned back towards the building, took a deep breath and plunged forward.

To his surprise, the door opened to his touch. As he entered, it slammed behind him, the noise echoing through the school's empty corridors and making him jump. Through glass doors ahead he could see an assembly hall, which seemed to be empty apart from a man wearing dark sunglasses and what looked like a bulky waistcoat. He was strutting nervously back and forth. As he crept closer to the glass, Aaron could see the children lying down, carpeting the floor from wall to wall. Many of them were silently crying; they stared at him as if pleading for help as he pushed open the doors and walked in amongst them, determined to show no fear. The man swung round to face him.

'Stop there!' he shouted, and Aaron could see that he was almost as terrified as the children on the floor. 'Don't move, or I will blow up the whole building!'

His hand had gone to a piece of string on his waistcoat, which Aaron guessed would be the trigger for the explosives that he could now see were packed around the man's back and chest.

As Aaron swung the Zeno gun up to fire, he saw that the charge light was red again. Something had gone wrong with the charging mechanism: he was facing the nervous bomber unarmed! Sweat prickled through his skin, and his legs felt like jelly. Then a squawking noise made both him and the bomber look up in surprise, and he saw Sophie the raven looking up at the man with interest. He realised that her wave-like nature had allowed her to pass through a slit in a window, something that would have been impossible for a particle.

'What is your name?' the raven called to him.

'I have no name, but I am a loyal soldier of the Supreme Ruler,' the man replied, squinting into the light, trying to work out who was speaking to him.

'Why do you want to kill these children, who are also the children of the Supreme Ruler?'

'Their faith in the Supreme Ruler is wrong,' the man

answered, and Aaron thought he heard a tremble of self-doubt in his voice. 'They deserve to die. It is written in the Book.'

The raven stretched her wings out, as if bored by the conversation already. 'Have you read the Book?' she asked casually.

'I have not read the Book myself,' the man admitted. 'But I have been taught by the people who sent me.'

'Many years ago,' the raven said, 'the Supreme Ruler gave the Book to all the Mushi, some of whose children are now lying at your feet. This was at a time when the rest of the world worshipped idols and did not even know about the Supreme Ruler, which is why breaking some of the commandments was punishable by death. But in actual fact, the whole Book was full of love for the people. The Supreme Ruler believed that people's relationships with each other were more important than their relationships to himself.'

'That is a lie,' the man shouted angrily. To Aaron it sounded as if he was as desperate to convince himself as much as the raven or anyone else. 'I have been told that everyone whose faith in the Supreme Ruler is wrong should be killed.'

'Your forefather,' the raven said in a chatty tone, as if the two of them were sitting around an evening camp fire discussing the finer points of world theology, 'whom some call Abraham and some call Ibrahim, did not use the sword to bring people to faith in the Supreme Ruler, but kindness and hospitality. That is what is actually written in the Book that you have not read.'

'I did not know that,' the man admitted, and Aaron could now see that he was struggling to fit what he was hearing with everything he had been taught since he was a small boy by the elders of his family and through the sermons of misguided priests.

'And that is not all,' Sophie continued. 'When the people decided to build a tower up to the heavens to fight the Supreme Ruler, he did not kill them, but merely scattered them.'

'Why?' the man asked, sounding genuinely interested now.

'Because they loved one another.'

Slowly, like a tree toppled by a woodsman's axe, the man sank to the floor as if all his strength had left him, along with his certainty, and his eyes filled with tears. Aaron moved forward cautiously as Sophie hopped silently nearer to them both. Aaron crouched down beside the sobbing man and put his arms gently around his shoulders, helping him to his feet, aware of the explosives in the waistcoat that were pressing against his own chest. Together they walked slowly and carefully out into the street, watched by the silent, anxious crowd. As they moved away from the building, parents ran inside in search of their little ones. The sound of crying rose from inside the building, but now they were tears of relief.

Aaron helped the man out of the waistcoat and then held it aloft to show the crowd that they were all now safe.

'Death to the terrorist!' shouted a lone voice, followed by another and another. The chant spread through the crowd as they realised their children were now safe and they had the upper hand over the man who had caused them so much fear. They began to advance on him. He simply stood where he was with his head bowed, as if surrendering to his fate.

'Stop!' Aaron stepped between them. 'Don't do this. He is sorry, and no harm has been done.' He turned to the man. 'By the way – now that you have changed your ways, you should choose yourself a name.'

After a moment of thought, the man said, 'From this day onwards, I wish my name to be Ibrahim.'

Sophie swooped down from the window of the school, calling to the crowd as she came. 'It was said that even a good man is not worthy to stand beside a sinner who is sorry.'

The crowd paused as they took in these words. They stepped back, and everyone relaxed. One man threw his hat into the air, shouting, 'Praise be to Aaron, our saviour!'

Another voice joined in and the chant gradually spread through the crowd. Aaron was overwhelmed and could not stop a proud smile from spreading across his face. He noticed that Sophie had flown high up into the clear sky above and was now out of earshot. He was free to bask alone in the glory.

'Yes,' he thought. 'I am their saviour. I have done very well indeed today.'

He closed his eyes to enjoy the feeling more intensely, which was why he did not see the Wasabi warriors until it was too late. The crowd did not hear their approach because of the noise they were making, praising the boy they now believed to be the saviour of their precious children. By the time Aaron realised what was happening the soldiers had already seized him. By the time the others realised what was happening, their friend and brother had been whisked away by the warriors. To the baffled crowd, it seemed that their hero had miraculously disappeared right in front of them.

A few hours after Aaron was taken prisoner, the Lord of Bravery returned to the throne room in the White Queen's castle and bowed low.

'Your Majesty, the chief of the Mushi tribe who eat salmon sushi is sending his nephew, Cassie, to us. I think we must receive him.'

'How will he enter the castle while we are besieged?' the Queen enquired.
'There is a secret underground passage,' Lord Bravery admitted. 'My people will show him the way. He will be here tomorrow.'

'A passage that is secret even from your Queen?'

She raised an eyebrow, amused by her loyal protector's embarrassment. 'Very well. Bring him to me when he arrives.'

The following day, when Cassie was shown into her presence, the Queen was struck by how handsome he was and by how dignified he remained even while bowing low to her.

'Forgive the intrusion, Your Majesty,' he said, 'but I have come to see you about an important matter.'

'I have been told that two strangers have come into our world to fight the Black Queen's leaders,' the Queen said. 'Apparently, they have already defeated one of them, and you have had something to do with this great achievement.'

'They have already defeated two of them, Your Majesty,' Cassie corrected her. 'But something unforeseen has occurred. One of the strangers, while in the dimension of evil, was taken away by Wasabi warriors and is now trapped.'

'What do you want me to do about this?' the Queen asked.

'My uncle proposes that you and your soldiers move

to the Cave of Good. You will be able to hold out for longer there.'

The Queen thought for a moment, then stood up and moved close to him, linking her arm through his and walking with him through the throne room.

'Many years ago,' she said, 'the army of the Western Mushi invaded the land of the tribe that does not eat shrimp sushi. They besieged the fortress called Casada. The defenders of the fortress resisted for three years, and then, when supplies ran out, they chose to kill themselves rather than surrender to the enemy. If I leave this castle, that would signify the final victory of the Black Queen. I will never do that. All is not yet lost, and the missing stranger may yet be found so that he can continue with this great mission.'

She slid her arm out of his and held out her hand for him to kiss, enjoying the sensation of his long, thick hair brushing against her extended wrist.

- The Land of Pride -

Not only had Aaron lost all track of time, he had lost all sense of space as well. The warriors had pulled a hood over his head as they bundled him away, which cut out all light and muffled most of the sounds. They tied his arms tightly to his sides so he could be more easily handled, which meant he was also unable to reach out and touch anything that might have given him a clue as to where he was. He drifted in and out of consciousness as he was bundled from one place to another. At one point he was thrown into a corner and left like unneeded luggage. He thought he heard the splashing of water; he felt a cool breeze and a rocking sensation, as if he might be going out to sea or crossing a lake in a boat, but he couldn't be sure of anything.

He heard muffled voices from time to time, but none of the words were clear to him until, without warning, the hood was ripped from his head. It took a moment for him to work out that he actually was in a boat, as he had thought, and that they were heading towards a brightly lit island in the centre of a dark lake. The blackness of the sky suggested that it was close to the middle of the night. Most of the island was covered by the most ostentatious castle he had ever seen. There were dozens of turrets and spires jostling to be the tallest or the most magnificent, all lit up to show off

their hundreds of windows and colourful domed roofs
to anyone who might be approaching across the water.

As the boat nosed its way towards the jetty, he saw
guards bustling out to meet it. They were all dressed
in gleaming white uniforms, covered in gold braid to
signify their importance. They even wore white gloves
as they helped his captors ashore. Everything seemed to
be designed to make sure visitors knew that they were
entering the domain of someone enormously important.
Two of the guards, carrying flaming torches, led Aaron
and the Wasabi warriors up a seemingly never-ending
staircase, which twisted round and round outside the
highest of the towers. With his arms still pinned to his
sides, Aaron struggled to keep his balance as they rose
higher and higher. He looked out over the black waters
of the lake, which appeared to stretch on forever. The
lights of the castle were reflected on its surface now
that the boat was docked, and the waters were still
again. Aaron's legs were aching from the effort of
climbing so many steps, but still he had to keep going,
prodded on by the impatient warriors.

When they reached the very top, they paused outside a
pair of golden doors. The guards released Aaron from the
ropes that bound him, since there was nowhere for him
to run to now apart from back down the staircase, which
was blocked by the warriors. Aaron shook his arms to
get the blood flowing once more. The white-uniformed
guards bowed low to him, as if he were now an

honoured guest rather than a prisoner, before opening the double doors to a fanfare of trumpets and ushering him through.

Inside was a gigantic staircase, sweeping down as far as they had just climbed up. It was wide enough for a dozen people to stand side by side, with marble balustrades carved in the shape of angels and thick gold carpeting. Way below, at the foot of the staircase, was a ballroom lit by a dazzling display of chandeliers. At its centre stood a man in a scarlet uniform, his chest covered in medals; his face sporting the biggest, twirliest moustache Aaron had ever seen. There were so many medals it looked like it must be an effort for him to hold himself upright, let alone puff his chest out so magnificently.

All around the edge of the hall were people wearing similar amounts of finery. As Aaron started his long descent to the celestial sound of trumpets, the crowd burst into applause, their medals and jewels sparkling in the lights as they raised their arms towards him. As he got closer to the bottom step, Aaron looked around in puzzlement, trying to work out what could possibly be happening.

The moustachioed man in the scarlet uniform held up his hand for silence, and the crowd immediately obeyed. The trumpets also fell silent as the man swaggered towards Aaron, his enormous sword

dragging on the floor behind him, and held out his gloved hand as if expecting it to be kissed. On the way down the staircase, Aaron had noticed that there were giant portraits of the same man, and relatives who looked very like him, all along the higher reaches of the walls. At ground level there were towering mirrors, designed to reflect the magnificence of all the guests and all the crystal and gilt that surrounded them.

'I am the great Lord of Pride,' the man announced, his chest seeming to swell even further, making the medals clank together. 'And I welcome you, Aaron, to my castle, which is without doubt the finest in the Land of the Mind.'

The crowd erupted again into cheers and applause at the magnificence of their surroundings and, by association, themselves.

'We've been watching you for a long time,' the Lord of Pride continued, once he had had enough of their cheering and silenced them with one imperious gesture. 'And today you have proved that you are worthy to become a Knight of Pride.' He turned to address the room at large. 'Many would tell us that pride is bad, that we should not be proud of what we do and what we achieve, and that we should instead remember that everything we have is given to us by the Supreme Ruler, including our talents and our achievements. But we know that is not the case...'

The crowd roared their approval of his words again. 'We have never seen this Supreme Ruler. We have no idea who he is or what he might or might not have given us. But we have our own selves. Everything that we do, we do ourselves, and we are rightly proud of that.'

There was more clapping as the Lord of Pride strutted back and forth before the crowd, drinking in their adoration before turning back to Aaron.

'Today you are being granted the honour of acceptance into our ranks, and you may remain with us forever.' He paused for dramatic effect. 'Do you, Aaron, agree to become a Knight of Pride?'

Aaron's brain was spinning so fast he couldn't understand anything clearly, apart from the fact that he knew he was in trouble. His hand reached out for the red button in his pocket, which would allow him to escape back to his old life. Then he thought about Stella and the importance of their mission, and he stopped short of pressing it. At least a thousand eyes were watching him, waiting to hear his reply, their hands raised ready to resume clapping and their voices to cheer once more.

Aaron pulled himself up to his full height. 'I will never,' he announced to the room, 'agree to be a Knight of Pride.'

After a few seconds of shocked silence, an offended rumble of anger rose from everyone's throats, growing into a chant. 'Disgraceful! Execute him! Remove his memory!'

The Black Queen's leader lazily raised his gloved hand, and the crowd quietened down again to a wounded grumble.

'According to the rules of the Order,' he declared, 'anyone who refuses the honour of becoming a Knight of Pride is given three days to rethink their decision and their false modesty. If, after three days, the candidate has not changed his mind, he will be subjected to a memory removal procedure and will be eternally exiled in the Black Queen's energy plantations. Take him away.'

Strong hands grabbed Aaron's arms once more and he was propelled from the room, away from the splendour of the gilt and glass through passages with plain stone walls, and dragged down yet more steps to the dungeons way below the castle. Aaron thought they might even be below the waterline of the lake. There, he was thrown into a cell lit only by one small, barred window high up above his head. The iron door slammed shut behind him and he heard the grinding of keys in the locks. He lay on the floor where they had thrown him for some time before pulling himself into a sitting position. There was no furniture, just a bare floor, some of it covered in water. Were they going to leave him here for the whole three days? he wondered. He felt his spirits sinking into despair and reached into his pocket once more to take out the red button. He put it on the floor beside him and stared at it hard, as if it might tell him what to do.

He had been there several hours and no longer knew if he was awake, or asleep and dreaming, when he heard a rustling noise above his head. He looked up to see that Sophie the raven had used her wave-like nature to penetrate the cell.

'Don't do it,' she said.

'Don't do what?'

'Don't press the red button. If you do, you will lose faith in your own strength forever and you will never achieve anything in life. The Supreme Ruler sends tests like this to everyone, without exception.'

'But what am I being tested for?'

'The Supreme Ruler wants you to reveal the qualities of your soul, qualities that even you do not know about, so that you can become stronger. By undergoing these tests you will rise up to a new spiritual level. Huge possibilities in life will open up to you and you will be on his radar forever. If you abandon the mission, the Supreme Ruler will forget about you and you will disappear permanently from his memory.'

'But what have I done wrong?' Aaron wanted to know. 'I haven't committed any crime.'

'You became proud,' Sophie replied, 'And that means you put yourself before the Supreme Ruler. But you must not despair. Almost everyone falls victim to pride at some stage in their lives. It is a sin that is very difficult to avoid. True humility has to be learned by most of us through hard lessons.'

'But why is taking pride in your achievement such a terrible thing? Didn't you feel proud for saving those children's lives, too?'

Sophie hopped off the windowsill and landed on the floor beside him, merging into the darkness. 'It was said that when the Supreme Ruler sends a soul into this world, it passes along a corridor. On the right-hand wall there is an inscription that reads, 'The whole world is created for you.' And on the left-hand wall there is one that says, 'Even the insignificant mosquito was created before you.' It is very difficult to find the right balance between these two walls.'

'You can say that again,' Aaron said. 'So what can I do? After all, the past can't be changed.'

'No, it can't. But it can be put right.'

'How?'

'Imagine you are holding a vase in your hands. You let go and it falls to the floor, breaking into tiny pieces. No law of physics prevents the pieces from following the process in reverse, putting themselves back together to reform the vase.'

'That has never happened,' Aaron scoffed.

'Exactly,' Sophie agreed, her beady eye glinting fiercely in the darkness. 'Such a process is highly unlikely. That is because of the great law which the Supreme Ruler gave to our world.'

'What is that law?'

'It states that in an isolated system, the level of visible chaos can either remain unchanged or it can increase. The broken pieces of vase have a significantly greater level of chaos than the whole vase. Scientists call this level of visible chaos "entropy". Nevertheless, all the pieces could be collected and stuck back together, and the vase could be restored to its original state. But doing this would use a lot of energy. You need to understand that evil possesses a much greater level of chaos than good. So it is not at all easy to move from a state of evil to a state of good.'

'So how can it be done, then?' Aaron asked.

'It requires a great deal of spiritual energy. A person must be sorry for his or her own actions and ask for the help of the Supreme Ruler. In the wise Book, it is written that anyone who wants to climb upwards will be given help. Anyone who wants to go downwards will not be prevented from doing so.'

'But I can do that for myself,' Aaron said, after a few moments' thought. 'I don't need the Supreme Ruler's help.'

'In order to defeat the Lord of Pride, you must first defeat the pride within yourself. A wise man once said, "Who is strong? It is not the person who captures an enemy city, but the person who conquers himself."'

It took Aaron a few seconds to realise that the raven had vanished, and he was alone again with his own thoughts and his own beliefs. Nothing disturbed the silence of the following two days apart from his jailers, who opened the door wide enough to push in a meagre portion of sushi every twelve hours. His thoughts went back and forth, merging at times into dreams as he slept fitfully on the hard floor. At other times he thought he saw hallucinations, but it was hard to tell reality from imagination. When he finally heard marching feet approaching the door, he made his decision.

'I believe the Supreme Ruler will not abandon me,' he
declared to the empty room, 'so I will fight until the end.'

He assumed the soldiers had come to fetch him, but
instead they threw open the door and pushed another
man in. The man stumbled and collapsed beside
Aaron. A single beam of light from the window fell
across his face, showing that this new companion was
old, with a high domed forehead and a bushy beard.
His eyes were kind, but tired, as if he had not been
allowed to sleep for a long time.

'Hello,' the old man said, pulling himself up into a
sitting position. 'Who are you?'

'My name is Aaron.'

'And how did someone as young as you get to be in a place like this, Aaron?'

Aaron told him his story. 'And who are you?' he asked, once he had finished.

'I am a scientist,' the old man replied.

'What sort of scientist?'

'Well, in my youth I showed some talent as a physicist, and one day I was approached by people in authority and asked to work on the development of a neuron bomb. I should have refused, of course, but like most scientists I was overcome with curiosity. I wanted to understand how such a thing could be achieved, and I didn't stop to think what the consequences of success might be. So many intriguing problems had to be solved and so many answers had to be found. It was an irresistible challenge.

'I wasn't the only one working on the project. It took us many years, but still it was only when our work was halfway to being completed that I realised I had done something terrible – that the bomb I was creating would be in the hands of the Mushi leader and that misfortune would come knocking on the doors of a great many people as a result. My conscience began to trouble me. I tried to fight the feelings and concentrate on the work, because I still wanted to solve all the puzzles and reach the conclusion, but in the end my conscience would not let me sleep at night or concentrate during the day, and so I refused to work on the project a moment longer.

'As a result, I was immediately banned from the laboratory and all Mushi were forbidden to give me work. With nothing else to do with my time, I wandered around the Land of the Mind, talking to the Mushi. I asked them questions that were sometimes unpleasant for them to think about, but their answers were always revealing, and many found their consciences awakening just like mine.'

'So why have they put you here, with me?' Aaron asked.

The old man gave a rueful smile. 'To be honest with you, Aaron, I became rather successful. My reputation spread all over the Land of the Mind, and I became proud as a result. That is how I came to be here.'

Aaron nodded. He understood exactly how easily that could happen. He thought for a few moments. 'So what, exactly, is a conscience?'

'When the Supreme Ruler tasked the ten Great White Rulers with governing the world, they entered into the soul of every Mushi. When the Black Queen took over, however, her leaders also entered the souls of the Mushi. The six Great White Rulers were imprisoned and surrounded by an almost impenetrable shell, so the Mushi could no longer hear them. They did not disappear completely, however, and it was possible, with a lot of time and a lot of deep thought, to pierce the shell and remember the lessons that the Great Rulers planted in our souls all those years ago. Those ten Great Rulers are the conscience that almost none of the Mushi can now hear.'

'Is there anything we can do?'

'It would be extremely difficult, but not impossible. The Great Rulers are imprisoned in a cave in the land of the Lord of Indifference. The Black Queen is so fearful that they might escape that she has made it virtually impossible for anyone to reach them. The cave is carved into a rock in the centre of the country and its only entrance is guarded by the Hundred-Headed Hydra of Indifference. The rock is also surrounded by a massive gorge that no one is able to cross.'

'So the situation is hopeless?' Aaron felt his spirits sink again.

'There is no such thing as a hopeless situation for the Supreme Ruler. When I was still working in the laboratory, a colleague of mine, whose name is Albert, calculated that somewhere a wormhole exists that would make it possible to reach the rock.'

'What's a wormhole?'

'It is a tunnel in space and time. With a wormhole, it is possible to travel instantly from one point in space to another, even if they are a huge distance apart. The rock could be reached through this wormhole, but it is only possible to pass through it in one direction. Whoever uses it must realise that there can be no return.'

'We have to give it a try,' Aaron said, without even a moment's thought.

'I agree.' The scientist stood up and stretched his aching joints. 'But first we must work out how to get out of here.'

The two of them set to thinking in silence. Several hours later, having come up with nothing useful, they heard the approach of running footsteps.

'They have come for me,' Aaron said, standing up and preparing to fight.

There was a clanking of keys and a grinding of locks and eventually the door flew open. Two Pride Guards

burst in – but to Aaron's astonishment, they threw off their hoods and embraced him.

'Guido! Ibrahim!' he exclaimed. 'How did you get inside the castle?'

'We managed to find a small boat and followed you across the lake,' Guido explained. 'Sophie was our guide. This castle was built for show, not for practical defence; it wasn't hard to get through the walls.'

'There were two guards asleep on duty,' Ibrahim continued, obviously excited by the adventure. 'We overpowered them and stole their uniforms. Come quickly, the boat is waiting. We have to get back across the lake and out of reach of the Lord of Pride.'

'This is my friend, the scientist,' Aaron said. 'He's coming with us.'

'I'm sorry.' Guido shook his head. 'That's impossible. The boat is very small – it can only take three people. If we tried to fit in a fourth, it would sink and we would all be drowned.'

A cackle of laughter made them all look up. There was Sophie the raven, back on the window ledge. 'In the temple of the Supreme Ruler,' she told them, 'there was a kind of magic. No matter how many people entered to worship him, there was always enough room.'

'I am not leaving this cell without him,' Aaron said, putting his arm around the old man's broad shoulders.

'Only a miracle will make that possible,' Guido said.

'Then we must hope for a miracle,' Aaron said. 'Lead the way.'

Ibrahim and Guido led them down a series of tunnels and staircases, the walls becoming increasingly damp as they got closer to the waters of the lake. They could hear angry shouting and running footsteps behind them, and knew that their escape had been discovered.

'Over here!' Guido shouted, pointing to a hole he and Ibrahim had made by removing bricks around a drain. They could only crawl through it one at a time, and the guards' footsteps were growing closer.

Outside, a small boat rocked gently on the surface of the water. There were indeed only three seats. As Ibrahim and Guido dropped down into the boat, a cloud of fog drifted across the water and enveloped them so that Aaron and the scientist could no longer see more than a few inches in front of their faces.

'We have to keep going,' the scientist told him, 'and have faith that we will make it.'

Guido and Ibrahim blindly stretched out their arms,

catching Aaron's hand and pulling him into the boat
beside them. Aaron then turned and held out his arms
in the same way, searching in the fog for the hand
of the scientist while Ibrahim and Guido set about
raising the sails.

As soon as he felt the old man's fingers, Aaron pulled,
just as the guards on the other side grabbed the
scientist's feet. Aaron heaved with all his might. The
scientist kicked at the men behind him, knocking
them backwards for just long enough. As he slid out of
the hole and into the boat, a wind sprang up, the fog
cleared and they could see that there were now four
seats. The same wind filled the sails with life and sent
the boat skimming over the water. Within minutes,
the angry shouts of the guards had disappeared into
the past.

- The Land of Betrayal -

When she realised her brother had vanished, Stella
fell to her knees, buried her face in her hands and
wept. All she wanted was to be safely back home with
her family, but she knew that if she pressed the red
button now, she might never see Aaron again. She had
to stay in the Land of the Mind until she had found
him again, but the thought of fighting on without him
was overwhelming.

Guido and Ibrahim, who were closest to her, both
knelt down and placed an arm around her shaking
shoulders.

'I will not rest,' Guido vowed, 'until I have found him and brought him back to you. I owe you and your brother everything, and I will do everything to repay that debt.'

'I will come with you,' Ibrahim said. 'If it had not been for Aaron's courage I, and all those innocent children, would be dead because of my ignorance. After what he was willing to do for me, I will now do everything I can to save him, too.'

'Come with us, Stella,' a kind voice said.

Turning her tear-stained face upwards, Stella found Erika looking down at her and an elegant hand outstretched towards her, offering to help her stand. As Guido and Ibrahim prepared to head off, a group of young people gathered around her, all apparently eager to be introduced.

'These are my people's council members.' Erika said. 'This is Josh and Valeb. This is Datlan and Aliram, and this is Miriam, Josh's fiancée.'

Even through her tears, Stella noticed that as Josh put his arm around the beautiful Miriam's shoulders and she affectionately slipped hers around his waist, young Datlan's coal-black eyes burned with a dangerous, unhappy-looking fire.

'You and your brother have helped to save many of our tribe today,' Erika continued. 'While we wait for these two to bring Aaron back, we would like you to come with us on our journey to our country, where someone of your strength is greatly needed.'

Stella thought for a moment. Part of her wanted to go and find Aaron, but part of her wanted to get to know Erika and her tribe better, and to help them on their journey if she could.

'Go with the tribe!' Sophie the raven's squawk interrupted her thoughts. 'It will help you to fulfil your mission.'

'Very well.' She picked up the sling and torch, took Erika's strong hand and stood up. Miriam let go of Josh and linked her arm with Stella's instead. Guido and Ibrahim disappeared in the opposite direction as the tribe loaded up their wagons and restarted their journey.

'When are you and Josh getting married?' Stella asked Miriam, after they had been walking some time.

'As soon as our people are able to return to their own land.'

'I think maybe Datlan likes you too, doesn't he?'

Miriam blushed prettily. 'It's clever of you to notice.

Yes, Datlan proposed to me some months ago, but I was already in love with Josh. It is very hard for him to see us together; I understand that. I hope he will meet someone else soon.'

By evening, the tribe and all their wagons had reached the edge of the desert.

'We will pitch our tents here,' Erika announced. 'The children need to rest. In the morning, when we are refreshed, we will set off once more.'

Stella watched in fascination as the people put up a village of tents with well-practised speed. They lit fires, then unpacked sushi without shrimp and laid it out. Erika invited Stella to join her by the fire outside her tent to share her meal.

'I'd love to hear more about your people,' Stella said, as it grew dark; soon, they could only see each other thanks to the flames of the fire.

'Of course.' Erika smiled, and Stella thought it was possibly the most beautiful smile she had ever seen. 'Many, many years ago, the Supreme Ruler gave us the Book, and we swore we would always be faithful to it. He led us into a country that was filled with energy and sushi and we lived happily there for many centuries, building the most beautiful temple to honour him. There were difficult times, where we

faced famines or wars, but he always protected us.
One day, a huge army invaded us from Western
Mushi. We were outnumbered a hundred to one and
were hardly armed at all, but still our people fought
bravely. In the end, however, we were crushed and
driven from the land that we had been given, and our
temple was destroyed. Each person and each family
had to survive in any way they could and we were
scattered all over the Western Mushi Empire. Some of
us even got as far as Eastern Mushi.'

'So how did you all get back together again?' Stella
asked. She glanced around at the many hundreds
of camp fires glowing in the night; the sound of
traditional songs rose up from around them.

'When we were driven out, the Supreme Ruler promised
us that he would not leave us in exile forever, and we
trusted him. Even though we were scattered far and
wide we retained our beliefs, our faith in his promise
and our feelings of solidarity. We also took the Book
with us into exile.'

'How did that help you?'

'Many nations have built fabulous empires,' Erika said.
'But sooner or later all material things are stolen or
destroyed. We had a spiritual empire because we had
the Book. No one could take that away from us because
it was in our memories, in our hearts and in our souls.'

'What is it like to live in exile?' Stella asked, thinking of how safe and happy she had always felt with her family at home.

'It's not easy,' Erika sighed. 'I'm not going to lie to you. Some of us did well for a while, but those good times always ended in long periods of persecution. People didn't like to see us prosper; it made them feel threatened. We were driven out of many countries, forced to abandon everything and leave, over and over again.'

'Why?' asked Stella, puzzled. 'Couldn't you have done something about it?'

'The only thing we could do was renounce the Book.'

'What does that mean?'

'If a member of the tribe said that he or she no longer believed in the Book, then they might eventually be accepted by those who hated and feared them, and their descendants might no longer be persecuted.'

'Did anyone do that?'

'A few did,' Erika admitted sadly. 'But most people stayed loyal to the Book, however difficult things got. Then there was a great disaster.'

'What was that?'

'A leader appeared in one of the regions of the Western Mushi. He was the Black Queen's most faithful servant and he promised her that he would exterminate all our people. Everyone – men, women, children.'

Erika stopped talking for a moment, her voice catching in her throat. Stella saw a tear glisten in her eye, a drop of gold in the reflected firelight.

'Did people renounce the Book then?' Stella whispered eventually. 'To save the tribe and themselves?'

'It was too late. Rejecting the Book meant nothing any more. Even if they had said they were renouncing it,

it would still have been in their hearts, and this leader understood that. The Black Queen was delighted by his offer, and so the decision was made to destroy us all. The extermination started immediately, and half our people were already dead before the good people among the Eastern and Western Mushi realised what was happening and got together to assassinate this man. We had cried out to the Supreme Ruler in our pain and he had heard us. Once the killing had stopped, the Supreme Ruler came to me in a vision and told me that now was the time for me to lead what remained of my people back to our land.'

'So is that where you are walking to now?' Stella asked, after a few moments' thought.

Erika nodded. 'It has been a hard journey, and it is
not over yet. That incident with Ibrahim, threatening
to kill our children – that sort of thing is always
happening to us, but it does not put us off. People can
always be helped to see the light. You saw how your
brother managed to persuade him to change. As long
as some of us are still alive, there is always hope.'

'May I continue the walk with you until you reach the
end of your journey?'

'Of course.' Erika put her arm round Stella's
shoulders and hugged her close. Only when she felt
the warmth of the hug did Stella realise how cold the
desert air had become without the sun's burning rays.

The following morning, the entire tented village
was dismantled and stacked back onto the wagons as
quickly as it had sprung up, and soon after dawn the
whole tribe was on the move once more. Sometimes
they walked in silence, lost in thought or prayer;
sometimes Erika would start them singing in order to
keep their spirits up as the heat of the day grew more
intense. Each day was the same: cold nights huddled
around camp fires, scorching hot days when the sand
dunes seemed to stretch before them to eternity. They
saw no other living souls apart from the occasional

scorpion scuttling for cover behind a rock, or vulture circling in the skies above.

Then, on the seventh day, a line of black-clad figures appeared across the horizon. At first Stella thought it was a mirage, brought on by the heat and exhaustion, but as they came closer she could see that it was real people. Thousands of them! As they drew nearer still, she could see that they were heavily armed, and their faces were not friendly. All the tribespeople around her had grown silent, their faces looking stubborn and determined.

'Who are they?' she whispered to Erika.

'That is the Mamalek tribe,' Erika replied, beckoning Josh and Valeb over. 'They hate us. They have fought against us ever since the Book was first given to us.'

'What shall we do?' Josh asked.

'I want you and Valeb to lead the defence,' Erika said.

'We are going to fight them?' Stella asked. 'But there are thousands of them, and they're all warriors! Half of your tribe is made up of children and old people.'

'Sometimes you have to fight, even if you know you are going to lose,' Erika said. 'If the Supreme Ruler wants us to reach our land, he will help us.'

'Then I will fight with you,' Stella said, pulling herself up to her full height.

Before they could say another word, the Mamalek charged towards them with blood-curdling screams, slicing down anyone who stood in their path. Josh and Valeb bravely rallied their own warriors to create a line of defence, and they even managed to strike down a few of the enemy; but every time one Mamalek warrior hit the ground, his blood staining the sand, five more rose up from the haze of the dunes behind to replace him. Erika fought as fiercely as any of the young trained warriors, cutting down every attacker who came near her sword. It was almost as though her belief gave her a special strength that made her untouchable.

Stella followed her lead, picking up an enormous sword from a fallen tribesman and running towards the enemy, swinging it wildly from side to side. As she focused on the swarm of oncoming warriors she noticed what looked like a wave of white rising up behind them, shimmering in the heat. The Mamalek didn't see their attackers coming from the rear until the last minute, and then had to turn to face them, leaving their backs undefended from the swords of the tribe.

More and more warriors in white joined the battle, appearing from every side as though they were rising up from the desert floor. Stella and her friends lowered their swords to watch as their attackers were forced to scatter and run in all directions.

When the last of Mamalek had gone or lay dead in the sand, the tallest of the white-turbaned warriors strode up to Erika and Stella, who were standing with Josh and Valeb.

'My name is Salakh,' he announced. 'I am the leader of these brave desert soldiers.'

'I've heard of you,' Stella blurted. 'We were told about you in the Cave of Good, but why have you decided to help us?'

Salakh beamed at her. 'Because the Supreme Ruler is for all the Mushi, and we all have to fight the Black Queen together.'

'Would you and your men join us in our journey?' Erika asked. 'We would be happy to provide food and nightly shelter in repayment for the great service you have done us today.'

'It is a kind offer,' Salakh smiled. 'But alas, we too are on a mission. The White Queen is in trouble. Her castle is surrounded by Wasabi warriors and we must go to her aid.'

Once they had watched their white-clad saviours disappearing back into the desert, the tribe returned to their routine of walking. The days continued to pass and their supplies of sushi began to run low. Hunger, thirst and exhaustion sapped the energies of the weaker members of the tribe, sometimes making it impossible for them to go on and forcing them to fall by the wayside.

One night, as Stella sat talking with Erika in her tent, they heard a commotion outside. Pulling back the flaps and stepping out, they found themselves face-to-face with a crowd of the tribespeople carrying burning torches. Datlan and Aliram were at the front.

'We have come to speak to you on behalf of the people.' Datlan spoke directly to Erika, pushing his face aggressively close to hers. 'You told us that the Supreme Ruler was revealed to you in a prophecy and commanded us to return to our lands. But we have been walking for months and our sushi energy supplies have run out. We have nothing left.'

'The Supreme Ruler has forgotten us.' Aliram stepped forward to support Datlan. 'We have to turn back and get out of the desert while some of us still have enough energy to make it. Otherwise we are all going to die in these sand dunes.'

Erika did not move. 'We are not going to do that,' she

said calmly. 'The Supreme Ruler never breaks his promises. We must trust him and continue onwards.'

Two wraith-like forms drifted out of the crowd, then appeared more solid in the flickering of the burning torches, and Stella remembered Salmon Mushi telling her about the dangerous ways of the Lords of Flattery and Self-Justification.

'You are a great, great people,' the Lord of Flattery cried out to the crowd. 'You deserve to be saved.'

'The Supreme Ruler has forgotten you,' the Lord of Self-Justification said. 'But the Black Queen has not. Three kilometres to the west of here there is a valley surrounded by mountains. There you will find plenty of sushi and energy sources waiting for you.'

'You deserve this reward for holding out so long,' the Lord of Flattery continued. 'You are such a special people. You need to rebuild your strength so that you can complete your epic journey.'

A buzz of excitement ran through the crowd. Someone shouted, 'We are saved!'

Miriam stepped forward and stood between Erika and Stella, facing the restless mob. 'You must not accept this offer,' she said. 'Our forefathers never rejected the Book, even when threatened by the sword, and they

are the reason that we are all still here. If you go to
the valley of the Black Queen you will be betraying
them and their memory. You will be betraying your
mothers, your fathers, your grandparents and all who
came before you.'

'Don't listen to her!' Datlan snarled angrily. 'She is
just trying to control your minds. They are all hungry
for power – Miriam, Erika, Josh and Valeb – every last
one of them! They are willing to sacrifice the rest of us
so that their names will be glorified and remembered
by future generations. We should execute them for
being willing to drive us to our deaths, and then we
should go to the valley of the Black Queen where we
will be welcomed and looked after. Enough of this
arrogant struggle in the name of some vision or other –
it's just a lie, created to fool us into following a dream!'

'Death to the traitors!' an anonymous voice chanted,
and others in the crowd joined in. They advanced
on Erika, fuelled by their empty bellies and aching
bodies. Stella could see they wanted someone to blame
for their desperate situation, someone to punish – and
Erika, standing tall and proud, was the obvious choice.
Josh and Valeb stepped forward, ready to protect their
leader with their own lives if necessary.

'Stop!' The word burst out of Stella so powerfully
that she could hardly believe she'd said it. The crowd
automatically came to a halt, looking confused. It

reminded her of the last time she had found this voice – when Marie had been in danger of having her memory eradicated by the red-hooded executioner.

'Your people have been slaves and wanderers,' she continued. 'They have been persecuted and killed, and now the Black Queen is luring the rest of you to your deaths. She is planning to finish the job that others have tried and failed to do before her. You must be patient. The Supreme Ruler will not abandon you.'

She still felt astonished at herself. She didn't understand how she had found such strength in her lungs, or the confidence to address a crowd with such authority, any more than she had understood it on the day she had saved Marie.

A woman stepped out of the crowd and stood a few inches away from her, towering over her. She had a small child in her arms and two terribly thin toddlers hanging onto her ragged skirts.

'It's easy for you to believe in the Supreme Ruler when you have energy!' she shouted angrily, pointing at Stella's energy counter. 'But my energy, and the energy of my children, will run out in two hours. What do you suggest we should do? Are you saying we should believe in the Supreme Ruler and lie down in the desert sand to die, just because you say so?'

Silence fell as everyone strained to hear Stella's reply. She lowered her eyes and looked at her energy counter. There were several green strips on it.

'I will give you my energy,' she said.

'And so will I,' Marie called out, stepping forward to stand next to Stella, her feet firmly apart and her arms folded bravely.

They both plugged their counters into those of the woman and her children, with connecting clicks which everyone could hear in the quiet of the desert night. The silent crowd watched in amazement as their counters began to fill. After a few minutes there was another click, then another and another. The sounds became louder and more frequent, until there was a steady buzz and the people realised that everyone's counters were filling with energy at the same time, even though they were not connected to any visible source.

'It's a miracle!' someone shouted, and others carried the shout through the crowd, repeating it and cheering as the energy flowed into them. 'We have energy! The Supreme Ruler has not forgotten us. We will carry on and return to our land!'

Datlan and Aliram stayed silent as they saw the mood of the people changing and felt its support ebbing

away from them. It was as if everyone had forgotten they were even there. Only Stella noticed as they exchanged glances, then stepped back out of the torchlight into the shadows of the night.

'Now, go and rest,' Erika told the crowd. 'We will set out in the morning with our renewed energy.'

The following morning, Stella was woken from a deep sleep by a wail of distress. When she ran outside, pulling on her clothes, she found Erika and Valeb comforting Josh.

'What's happened?' Stella asked, as Marie joined her, too. Erika looked at them with deep sorrow in her eyes.

'After everyone had gone back to their tents last night,' she said, 'Datlan and Aliram kidnapped Miriam.'

'What! Where have they taken her?'

'To the valley of the Black Queen, we think. We're going after them.'

'We will come with you,' Stella and Marie said at once.

'Well, we have to hurry,' Erika said. 'Once they're in the valley we won't be able to follow them. We will die if we enter the realm of the Black Queen.'

The five of them ran faster and longer than any of them thought they could. Just as they reached the entrance to the last ravine they saw the two men up ahead, pulling Miriam behind them on a rope, as if she were an animal they were taking to market.

Enraged by the sight, Josh set off again, ignoring the cries of the others warning him to wait. Seeing that he simply couldn't listen to reason, Stella ran after him, throwing herself at his legs and knocking him to the ground. The others quickly joined her, helping her to pin him down.

'It's too late,' Stella told him. 'We can't go in there. We will have to think of another way to save her.'

Realising that she was right, Josh curled into a ball on the ground and sobbed uncontrollably, repeating the same words over and over again. 'What will they do to her? What will they do to her?'

'Look,' Stella said, pointing into the ravine.

A line of Wasabi warriors had appeared in front of Datlan and Aliram, ordering them to stop. Miriam collapsed to her knees, exhausted; her face was red and streaked with tears. A general stepped forward to speak, his words carrying back across the landscape.

'Which of you is prepared to enter willingly into the service of the Black Queen?' he demanded.

'I am,' replied Datlan.

'I am,' echoed Aliram.

'Then you shall be made Wasabi warrior generals and will serve with us.' He walked over to Miriam and prodded her with his foot, forcing her to look up at him. 'And you?'

'Never,' she spat back at him.

'In that case,' the general declared in a bored voice,

'we sentence you to memory removal and exile in the Black Queen's energy plantations.'

Two warriors stepped forward and placed a helmet on her head. Within seconds, she had disappeared, and the rope that had been holding her fell limply to the ground.

Josh let out a cry of anguish. Erika knelt beside him, cradling his head in her arms. 'I understand your pain,' she said, stroking his face, 'but the Supreme Ruler is just. He will punish the traitors and you, I believe, will be reunited with the one you love.'

After a while, Josh pulled himself up to his feet. The group walked silently back to the camp, where the others had already taken down the tents in preparation for another day's march.

The two remaining rulers in the Black Queen's castle were watching as the energy flowing in continued to slow. Their shoulders stooped, they were clearly feeling discouraged by the way things were going.

'Don't look so negative,' the Black Queen snarled. 'Everything is about to change. We have just acquired two new generals who will finish off young Aaron and Stella once and for all.'

- The Zone of Indifference -

As the boat glided along the shoreline of the lake, the four escapees from the Castle of Pride were lost in thought, all trying to take in what had just happened.

Eventually the scientist spoke. 'You and your friends saved my life,' he said to Aaron. 'And I would like to stay with you to the end of your mission, in case there is anything I can do to help you in return.'

Aaron nodded his thanks, and returned silently to his own churning thoughts. After travelling across the water for some hours, they spotted a light on the shore and made their way towards it. Once the boat had ground to a halt, they found the phi-flyer and Sophie the raven waiting for them with some celebratory sushi and drinks laid out on long tables.

Both Aaron and the scientist ate hungrily – they had been starved of anything more than stale bread for days. Once they were ready to take their seats, the phi-flyer hummed off and they settled back in the comfort of the cushions. All of them fell asleep within seconds.

When they eventually woke, they had reached their next destination. The on-screen message read: 'Zone of Indifference. Weapons: the spear of compassion and three Gamma knives.'

'What's a Gamma knife?' Aaron asked.

'It is a device that produces very high-energy gamma radiation,' the scientist explained. 'The energy is so high that it can cut through any object as easily as a hot sword through butter.'

As they left the phi-flyer, the scientist picked up the spear while Aaron, Guido and Ibrahim took a Gamma knife each. Outside they found themselves on a road.

'We need to find Albert,' the scientist announced, immediately setting off at a fast pace. 'Only he knows where the wormhole is located.'

'Who is Albert?' Guido asked as the others hurried behind, trying to keep up.

'A colleague of his,' Aaron explained. 'The scientist believes he has the answers we need.'

'And what is a wormhole?' Ibrahim panted, his thick glasses sliding down his nose as he started to sweat.

'I'll explain later,' Aaron replied. 'It's a bit complicated and I'm not sure I totally understand yet.'

He picked up speed and caught up with the scientist. 'How will you find Albert?' he asked.

'I know where he lives,' the scientist replied, without slowing his pace or taking his eyes off the horizon. 'I will take you there.'

They reached a town, but their spirits sank as they looked around. Every building was dirty and broken down. In some cases the roofs had completely caved in, leaving skeletons of rafters sticking up into the sky. But there were still signs that people lived amidst the ruins. A beggar holding a sign which read, 'I have nothing to eat' silently waved a mug at them, but no coins rattled inside it and he didn't bother to speak or catch their eye. Aaron wished he had something he could give him, but the man didn't seem to care. A little further down the same street they saw an old woman carrying

a heavy pack on her back. As they watched, she tripped
on a pothole and fell heavily to her knees. Even though
she was crying out and bleeding, trapped under the
weight of the pack, no one took any notice. Aaron
ran over and helped her up. She glanced at him in
surprise, shrugged and hobbled away.

Aaron had to run to catch up with the scientist again as
they entered a small square. There were a lot of people
sitting around, and on the far side two big brutish men
were beating a small child viciously; but everyone was
ignoring them. Ibrahim rushed across and dragged the
men away from the child, then gave them a taste of
their own medicine. They shrugged and walked away as
if his angry blows had barely touched them. The child

also limped away, drying his tears on the back of his hand without a word of thanks.

'You are both wasting your energies,' the scientist told them. 'I've been here before. In this zone, nobody cares about the sufferings of anyone else or even of themselves. No one helps anybody, and nobody expects to be helped.'

'That's a terrible way to live,' Aaron said. 'Can't we do something to change it?'

'In order to defeat evil,' the scientist said, 'it is not enough to fight what results from it. You have to destroy its source within a person's soul. If we defeat the Hydra and release the six Great Rulers, we will be doing just that.'

They walked on for another hour through the dirty, broken streets until they reached a small crumbling house down an alley. A pack of feral dogs seemed to be guarding it as they rummaged through piles of litter in search of scraps. The dogs growled threateningly at the travellers without bothering to raise their snouts from the dirt as the scientist knocked loudly on the rotting door. A woman came to open it, but she could barely shift it on its broken hinges. When her timid face was eventually visible through the crack, they could see that she was crying.

'I am a friend of Albert's,' the scientist told her. 'Is he in?'

'Are you the scientist?' she asked, wiping her face on the stained sleeve of her shirt.

'I am.'

'He told me you would be coming before they took him away.'

'Who took him away?'

'One of his colleagues reported him for caring, and they came to arrest him.' Just saying the words started her weeping again.

'Did he ask you to give me anything?' the scientist asked.

'Oh, yes.' The woman forced the door open a few more inches, just enough for the visitors to be able to squeeze through, and went to a drawer in a broken table. She took out a package and handed it over.

The scientist unwrapped it to reveal a small computer. 'What is this for?' he asked. 'Did he say anything to you about a wormhole?'

The woman sank into an armchair and Aaron noticed several mice making a hurried escape from under the cushions. She took a deep breath as she tried to remember the details. 'Just before he was arrested he was sitting at that table, drawing something that looked like a map. When the police burst in, they grabbed him and the map at the same time.'

'What should we do?' Aaron asked.

'We need to free Albert from prison,' the scientist said.

'But we need to know where he is. Stay here, and don't open the door to anyone until I return.'

A few hours later, the scientist was back. 'I've found him,' he announced, once they'd let him in. 'He's in the central prison. The window of his cell is on the first floor. There's a grill over it, but I think it's big enough for a man to get through. There are Mushi police patrolling the perimeter.'

'So, how are we going to free him?' Aaron asked.

'We'll cut the bars with a Gamma knife. It can cut anything. We'll also need a ladder. It will be risky – if we're caught, we'll end up in the cells ourselves. Or worse.'

'We have no option,' Aaron said, glancing at Guido and Ibrahim. They nodded agreement, their faces grim.

'There's an abandoned barn behind the house,' the woman told them. 'You'll find a ladder in there, although it's probably broken.'

Guido and Ibrahim went to explore, and returned with a wooden ladder. Several rungs were missing and many of the surviving ones looked rotten, but it was something, at least.

Once darkness had fallen they set out on their mission, grateful that no one had bothered to mend the broken street lamps. It was slow going as they picked their way over the potholes in the dark and carried the ladder awkwardly around corners, trying to ignore the splinters that the crumbling wood left in their hands.

Eventually they arrived beneath the walls of the prison, and the scientist pointed out Albert's window. 'I'm the lightest,' Aaron said, 'so I should go up and cut the grille. One of you needs to hold the ladder while the other two look out for guards.'

The scientist took a firm grip of the ladder while Guido and Ibrahim headed in opposite directions to keep watch. Aaron started to climb, gingerly testing the strength of each rung before putting his full weight on it. One or two gave way beneath his feet, and he could feel splinters stabbing into his thin shoes as he cautiously made his way up. Once he got to the top, he started to work on the bars with the knife.

'Mushi guards!' Ibrahim called out as two policemen appeared around a corner, brandishing neuron pistols and sounding the alarm.

'Work faster!' the scientist cried up to Aaron.

Ibrahim and Guido leapt upon the policemen
and overpowered them, wrenching their weapons
from their hands. But just as Aaron cut through
the last bar, the street was flooded with light, and
the deafening scream of sirens blasted from every
direction. From his vantage point on the ladder,
Aaron could see a force of more Mushi police
assembling around the corner, preparing to attack.
He turned his attention to the gloom of the room
inside the window, where he could see a thin young
man with a wild beard and hair cowering in the
corner.

'Come quickly,' Aaron shouted. 'We are your friends!
The scientist is with us.'

The young man hesitated for a second, as if weighing
Aaron up, then did as he said and followed him down
the ladder. More rungs gave way beneath their weight,
and then, just as Albert reached the bottom, the whole
thing broke apart and pieces of rotten wood rained
down on top of them.

Albert's face lit up with relief when he saw his old
colleague again, and the scientist gave him a big hug.
But there was little time for greetings as the police
force came crashing around the corner with their
weapons drawn.

'Take us to the wormhole!' the scientist shouted. 'Fast!'

They ran as hard as they could, but the police kept chasing – even when they left the town and plunged into the surrounding forest, dodging between the trees and tripping over the tangled undergrowth in the dark. The splinters in Aaron's feet were agony, but he just had to push on.

'The wormhole is just ahead,' Albert shouted. 'But we need to slow the police down. Use your knives to fell some trees – we'll quickly make a barricade. And give me the Mushi neuron pistols. I'll hold them off while you get to the wormhole. If I succeed, I'll meet you over there.'

There was no time to argue. They quickly felled the trees and left Albert with the captured pistols. They could hear shooting and the cries of the injured as they ran the final few hundred metres. Ahead of them was a huge iron door with a green button beside it, which the scientist pressed.

The door opened, and a narrow, well-lit tunnel threw a blanket of dazzling light over them. As soon as all four of them were inside, the door shut behind them with a mighty, echoing boom, as if they had just gone through the sound barrier. Now they just had to keep going forward until they came to another door. This one had a screen on it and another green button beside it. Again, the scientist pressed the button, and a message appeared on the screen:

```
                  Attention.
     Entry to the wormhole requires
     a ten-digit password. If you do
       not give the correct password
     within ten minutes, the wormhole
       will be closed and destroyed.
```

'We'll never work it out in time!' Aaron cried, aware suddenly of just how much his feet and hands were hurting from the splinters. Guido and Ibrahim sank to the floor, their heads in their hands.

'All is not lost,' the scientist said, opening the mini-computer that Albert had left for him at the house. His fingers flew over the keys, his brow furrowed with concentration as he tried to work out the most likely combination of digits. A clock on the screen started ticking down from ten minutes.

Back at the barricade, Albert was firing the pistols so fast that the police never imagined for a moment that there was only one person holding them up. The energy dials on the guns soon began flashing red, and after a few moments the police chief realised that all the gunshots were now coming from his own men.

'Cease fire!' he ordered, and a terrible silence fell over the forest. 'They are out of energy. Charge the barricade.'

As they came over the top of the trees they saw Albert, curled into a ball, waiting to be beaten and recaptured. 'He's on his own,' a policeman said. 'The others must have made it to the wormhole.'

The police chief prodded Albert with the tip of his boot. 'It is all over, my friend,' he sneered. 'Your friends will be lost forever in the wormhole. Tomorrow your memory will be removed and you will be despatched to the Black Queen's energy plantations.'

The police chief then made a strange gurgling sound. When Albert dared to peep, he saw that a silently delivered arrow had passed through the man's throat. After a few seconds of struggling for breath, he toppled to the floor. A thousand more arrows followed. Albert curled himself back up into a tight ball as the Mushi police span around, trying to spot their attackers, falling to the ground one after another as the arrows found their marks. When the last of them was lying still in the undergrowth, the arrows ceased and another group of soldiers with green bandanas tied around their heads emerged from behind the trees. They moved silently among the bodies, checking that they were dead and taking their weapons. Their leader, who wore a royally embroidered green and gold coat, made his way over to Albert and extended his hand.

'My name is Arthur,' he said, helping Albert to his feet. 'I am the commander of the Resistance Army. You must not stay here – more Mushi will arrive soon. You must come with us.'

Albert was only too happy to put himself under the protection of such a ferocious and effective fighting force. 'Where are we going?' he enquired.

'We are on our way to help the White Queen.'

'Then I'll be delighted to travel with you,' Albert said.

Back at the door to the wormhole, eight minutes had passed. The scientist continued to work on the computer while the other three hardly dared breathe for fear of distracting him. Each time he tried a wrong number, the screen rejected it with an ugly sound. The tension was almost unbearable. Another minute passed, and Aaron glanced down at his red button. If he pressed it now he could get safely away from all this danger. He felt so tense it seemed like his head was exploding. But how would he ever be able to explain to people why he had left his friends to face danger without him? How would he live with himself? On the other hand, if he died in the wormhole, he would never see his parents or his grandparents again. And maybe Stella had already pressed her red button and was waiting at home for him. All these thoughts rushed through his head, but he also remembered the words of Sophie the raven: 'Even when a sword is hovering over your head, continue to trust the Supreme Ruler.'

Then another voice echoed through his memory – that of Salmon Mushi: 'According to ancient legend, children who eat sushi in amounts that correspond to the Supreme Ruler's number will be able to bring back the Book.'

There were now only thirty seconds left to find the correct combination.

'The Supreme Ruler's number is phi!' Aaron shouted. 'Try that!'

The scientist immediately understood, and with trembling fingers began to enter the first digits – 1.618...

'Faster, faster!' the others urged.

As he pressed in the last digit there were just five seconds to go. No time to try again. The friends all froze, staring at the door for what seemed like forever.

And then a message flickered up onto the screen:

Password correct.

They'd done it! The door swung open, and they made their way through. As it slammed behind them there was a moment of total blackness, and then the light reappeared like a stormy orange dawn and they found themselves standing on a plateau on top of a large rock. The abyss all around was so deep it was impossible to see the bottom, but in front of them a formless mass was seething and pulsating, emitting terrible roaring sounds from a hundred angry mouths. In the centre of this mass something red pulsed, like the crater of a volcano, or maybe an open wound.

'This is the Hydra of Indifference,' the scientist told them in an awed whisper. 'It can only be defeated within the heart.'

'Then we will head for the heart of the Hydra,' Aaron said, and they all took several tentative steps forward.

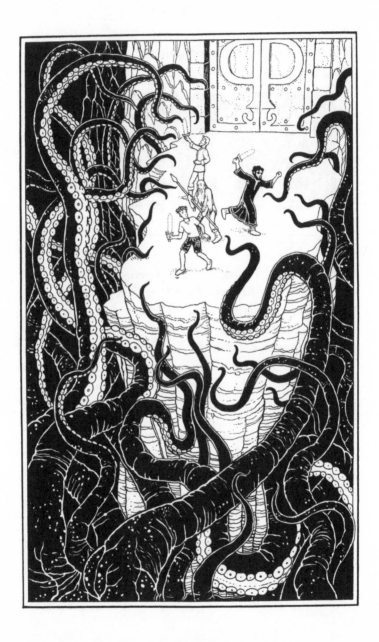

A thousand black tentacles protruded from the undulating body. As they drew close she lashed out, trying to snatch them all up and toss them into the waiting abyss. As fast as Aaron, Guido and Ibrahim slashed the tentacles off with their Gamma knives, new ones grew back in their place.

As he chopped and struggled, Aaron noticed in despair that his Gamma knife was running out of power. When the next tentacle flashed in his direction, there was nothing he could do. The tentacle wrapped itself around him, lifting him triumphantly into the air. Everything inside his head was spinning as he prepared himself to be hurled into the void below.

But the scientist had noticed just in time, and clambered up the rock face above the Hydra, the Spear of Compassion in hand. He took careful aim and launched the spear from the clifftop directly into the blood-red heart of the Hydra. A fearful explosion engulfed them all in choking black smoke... and once it cleared, a burst of sunshine revealed that the Hydra had gone. In her place was a green meadow stretching across to the mouth of a cave, with a locked door across its entrance. But the lock had a key poking out of it, as if inviting them to enter.

'The six Great White Rulers are inside that cave,' the scientist said. 'You should unlock the door and release them. This is the single greatest moment in the history of the Land of the Mind.'

'No.' Aaron bowed, gallantly extending his arm to the scientist. 'You have brought us here – the honour should be yours.'

'Very well.' The scientist accepted the offer graciously and walked slowly and ceremoniously forward, then turned the key with exaggerated movements and pulled open the door. A bright light appeared behind them; they turned and saw that the phi-flyer had arrived.

'It's time,' Aaron said.

All four of them climbed in and sank into the waiting seats with deep sighs of relief.

Inside her castle the White Queen looked up at the walls and allowed herself a small smile as the portals through which she was connected to her Great White Rulers flickered back on. The static began to clear; the energy flow increased and their faces came into focus one by one.

- Despair -

The tribe had been walking through the scorching
desert all day when Erika called a halt for the night.
As soon as they had set up camp and eaten, everyone
fell into an exhausted sleep. There was no sound apart
from the desert breezes drifting over the sand.
Then Josh woke up. There was something lurking
inside his tent. The only light came from the dying
embers of the fire outside, but that was just enough to
reveal the hideous intruder as it rose up from the floor
and hovered over him, dripping with menace. It leapt
on him, pinning him down with painfully sharp claws.

'Who are you?' Josh demanded, unable to move.

'I am Moloch, the messenger of the Demon of the Desert.'

'What do you want from me?'

'The Black Queen has ordered my master and his armies to destroy your people. But you can avoid that fate.'

'How?' gasped Josh.

'Turn back, and you will be spared.'

'We will never do that,' declared Josh with all the defiance he could muster from his helpless position.

'Then tomorrow you will all die.' Moloch took obvious delight in the prospect.

'A great man once said that a nation that dies fighting will be reborn,' Josh managed to say. 'Whereas a nation that surrenders will disappear. A nation can be weakened and damaged, but it will never be fully destroyed until its spirit is broken.

'Many years ago, when our forefathers lived in our land, a large army of Western Mushi attacked and occupied our country. Our forefathers rebelled against them. Many said that the rebellion was doomed; they were outnumbered and outgunned. And the rebellion did indeed fail. All the rebels were killed, but their heroism strengthened the spirit of our nation, and we remember them to this day.'

But Moloch ignored him. 'If you turn back,' he growled, 'the Black Queen, in her great mercy, will return Miriam to you.'

The creature then stood back, knowing he had sown seeds of doubt in the young man's mind. Josh sat up, then stayed very still, staring straight ahead as the conflicts battled it out inside his head.

'I love Miriam more than life,' he said eventually, 'but I cannot take my love from the hands of the queen of evil.'

On hearing these words, Moloch gave a great roar of frustration and vanished into the blackness, making the embers of the fire outside flare up angrily as he passed.

The next morning, Josh said nothing to the others about the visitation in the night. He hoped it had perhaps been a particularly vivid dream, or a hallucination brought on by exhaustion and grief. After walking for a few hours, however, people started to murmur, gazing at the sky, which was turning a dramatic shade of red. And when Josh saw creatures appearing on the horizon, he knew that he hadn't imagined anything.

'They are the demons of the desert,' he told Valeb. 'We need to organise everyone into battle formation.'

As Josh and Valeb prepared the tribe to defend itself, Stella, Erika and Marie waited for their chance to fight alongside them. The army of demons was moving slowly towards them. They were not in any hurry, no doubt because they were sure of their fighting skills, and knew that the tribe was outnumbered – they were confident they would win. At the front was the mighty Demon of the Desert, with the lower-ranking demons and their countless hordes of horror close behind. Electrical impulses buzzed and crackled from their eyes, setting fire to anyone or anything they struck as they reached the front lines of the tribe. The tribe's soldiers fought with all their hearts, but for every demon they shot, ten more surged forward; they were dying like flies.

'Our energy is running out!' Josh shouted to Erika and Stella over the noise of the battle. 'In an hour's time, we will have no firepower at all.'

Stella looked up at Sophie the raven who had appeared in the air above her, out of reach of the demons. 'What should we do?' she called.

'Take the sling you brought with you from the phi-flyer,' the raven advised, 'and give it to Josh. If he can hit the Demon of the Desert on the head with it, you will win.'

Stella ran to Josh and gave him the sling, telling him what Sophie had said.

Josh nodded and called Valeb over. 'Take the strongest soldiers and attack the Demon from the right,' he instructed. 'I will come in from the left.'

'But we will all die!' Valeb protested.

'Trust me,' Josh said. 'There is no other way.'

Valeb shook Josh's hand as if to say farewell, then went immediately to choose ten strong soldiers who he knew would be willing to give their lives to save the tribe.

Doing their best to protect themselves with shields, and firing with the last of their neuron pistols' energy, Valeb and his soldiers attacked the Demon from the right-hand side. The Demon shot them down with electrical impulses, laughing at how stupid they were to expose themselves like that. He was so busy picking them off one by one that he didn't see Josh moving up stealthily from the left.

Within a minute, Valeb was the only one of his group
left standing. He dodged back and forth, weaving
from side to side to keep the Demon concentrating on
taking aim. He could see how close Josh was getting
on the other side. Perhaps he flicked a glance towards
Josh's position, giving him away, because the Demon
swung round just in time to see him swinging the
sling around his head.

Valeb hurled his shield at the back of the Demon's
head. The Demon swung back with a bellow of
anger and swiped Valeb hard with a claw, sending
him spinning backwards and killing him before
he had even hit the ground. Then he turned back
to deal with Josh, but the stone was already on its
way from the sling – going so fast that not even a
demon could dodge it. It hit him square in the head
and he exploded like a bomb – and all the lesser
demons vanished in the explosion, just as Sophie had
predicted.

The rest of the tribe looked sadly at Valeb and his
soldiers lying dead on the ground.

'We will always remember their sacrifice, but now we
must carry on,' Erika announced to the exhausted
crowd around her. 'Our land is not far away now.'

The tribe walked on for two more days, which drained almost all their energy. And then, early the next morning, before they could even start out, a sandstorm whipped in from the far end of the desert. The grit-filled winds knocked the people off their feet, covering them in sand if they didn't manage to get straight back up again. Walking would be impossible, as they could no longer see where they were going; all they could do was huddle together for protection.

'The people are close to despair,' Josh told Erika and Stella. 'They don't believe their energy will hold out long enough for them to reach their land.'

'Once the storm has passed, we have to keep going,' Erika said. 'There's no alternative.'

With a scarf pulled up to protect her nose and mouth, Stella gazed at the swirling sands. 'What are those?' she asked, pointing at some black spots approaching over the wind-swept dunes.

Erika turned to see what she meant. 'We are doomed,' she replied. 'Those are the scorpions of despair. And we do not have the energy to defeat them.'

Stella's heart sank, but she tried to be brave.

'We will remain standing to the last man, woman or child,' she said. 'And until the last moment.'

Helpless, the people stood and watched as the scorpions moved closer, waving their huge, vicious pincers in the air.

Then Stella remembered the words of Salmon Mushi: 'You may appeal to the Supreme Ruler three times.' She raised her arms into the wind and called out silently, 'Oh, Supreme Ruler, this nation has obeyed you and walked almost all the way to their land. Please don't abandon them now. Don't allow them to die in the desert.'

But the scorpions kept coming, and the leader was raising his pincer high, ready to strike.

'Stella,' Erika shouted, 'I have just had a vision. Do you still have the torch of hope you brought from the phi-flyer?'

Stella frantically plunged her hand into her pack, but couldn't find the torch. With a surge of panic she remembered that she had left it in her tent, which was twenty or thirty metres away; she couldn't possibly reach it in time.

And then something incredible happened. Marie ran from behind her towards the tent.

'Stop, you'll die!' shouted Stella, but Marie paid no attention. As the claw of the scorpion bore down on her friend, Stella closed her eyes in terror. When she opened them again, Marie had managed to reach the tent and was running back with the torch in her hand. As the scorpion grabbed her and lifted her up towards its waiting jaws, she threw the torch to Stella.

Stella lit the torch and everything was bathed in a magical, golden light. The sandstorm subsided with a deep sigh and the scorpions faded away like a bad dream. Stella held the torch high, feeling her spirits soar, and seeing the same excitement and anticipation in everyone around her.

They packed up with lighter hearts, and as they moved on, the desert slowly grew green around them. Mountains rose up, their peaks soaring into the white clouds above. The valley ahead of them was filled with sushi energy sources.

'This is our land!' Erika said, her eyes wide with wonder and edged with tears of joy. 'Stay here with us, Stella, and we will make you our queen.'

'Thank you so much!' gasped Stella. 'I'm honoured, I truly am, but I must find Aaron and complete our mission.' And at that moment, the phi-flyer appeared in the sky above them.

As Stella and the tribe were battling the scorpions and the sandstorm, Albert, Arthur and his forest soldiers were marching across a broad plain.

'You have so much knowledge,' said Arthur to Albert. 'So how do you think we can change our world for the better?'

'Through science,' Albert replied, without a second's hesitation. 'Science drives progress and improves the lives of everyone.'

'But the Supreme Ruler has given us free will – the freedom to do good or evil. Science doesn't take sides – it can be used to further the cause of either of them.'

'Of course,' Albert said. 'That's true. So how do you think can we improve our world?'

'We must unite science with the Book. Only then will we be able to improve our world and destroy evil.'
As Arthur spoke, a small army, all dressed in white, appeared ahead of them.

They stopped and reached for their weapons, but then Arthur realised who it was. 'It's Salakh and his army!' he exclaimed. 'Just in time for us to join forces and save the White Queen.'

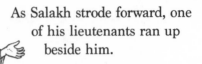

As Salakh strode forward, one
of his lieutenants ran up
beside him.

'O, Salakh,' he said.
'Everyone knows of
your bravery and
valour, but we are
about to unite our forces
and throw our lot in with
Mushi who believe in the
Supreme Ruler in a different way
to us. Are you sure this is the right thing to do?'

'You're right,' Salakh answered. He put his hand
on the man's shoulder, but did not slow down. 'Our
beliefs do differ, but the Supreme Ruler is the same
for all of us. And as you can see, the Black Queen
does not discriminate either.'

As they came together, Arthur and Salakh embraced
warmly. And then the two armies merged to continue
their journey, with every warrior, both white and
green, embracing and cheering one another joyfully.

Towards evening, they arrived at the entrance to a
narrow gorge with sheer cliffs on either side. They
decided to camp there for the night as the cliffs would
protect them from surprise attack. In the morning,
before setting off, they sent scouts to the northern end

of the gorge, but they returned within a few minutes.

'An army of Wasabi warriors is blocking the gorge,' they reported. 'We cannot get through that way.'

'Then we will go back,' Arthur said, 'and try another way.'

They hurried to the southern mouth of the gorge, but that too was now blocked by Wasabi warriors.

'We're trapped,' Salakh said. 'What shall we do, Arthur?'

'We must not surrender,' Arthur replied. 'We will attack them from either side and get through or die trying.'

'There is another possible solution,' a voice said from behind them. They swung round to stare at Albert.

'And what's that?' cried Arthur and Salakh, at the same time.

'I could try to work out the location of a tunnel that would get us out of here.'

'What kind of tunnel?'

'A quantum tunnel. Our country is subject to quantum laws, which are different to the laws of the ordinary world. For instance, if you hold a ball in your hand in the ordinary world, then roll it up a slope, the ball will not go over the top to the other side if you don't use enough force. It won't have enough energy – it will roll back down. In a quantum world, though, everything is different. Even if the energy level isn't high enough, a certain quantity of quantum particles – electrons, for example – will still go over the top of the hill. This is called the quantum tunnelling effect. If we can work out the location of the quantum tunnel, we can enter it and end up on the other side of the mountain.'

Arthur and Salakh exchanged puzzled looks, but they were willing to give it a try.

'Let's begin work at once, then,' Salakh said. 'Our fate is in your hands.'

Albert nodded absent-mindedly, as if he willingly accepted the responsibility and was confident he could do it. He found a pencil and paper in a deep inner pocket of his coat and began making complicated calculations. An hour passed, and then another, without him even looking up.

Then a scout's voice rang out. 'The Wasabi are attacking – from both sides!' he cried.

'Albert,' Arthur said, 'should we prepare to fight?'

'Yes, yes,' Albert said, still without looking up. 'It's always good to prepare for the worst.'

Both leaders signalled to their men to prepare for battle. Amidst the clattering of weaponry and the thunder of running boots Albert worked on with his calculations. The bloodcurdling shouts of the enemy were only metres away when he sprang to his feet with a triumphant yell.

'I've found it. Follow me!'

He ran to the foot of the mountain and placed his hand on a grey stone that was sticking out. The others, waiting behind him, watched in amazement as part of the mountain moved away, creating an opening the size of one person. The enemy was now engaged with the first line of defence, the din of battle drowning out the rumble of the mountain opening.

'Follow me!' Albert shouted again, squeezing through the gap.

All Salakh and Arthur's soldiers who were not already actively fighting followed. As soon as the last one was through, the mountain closed up once more. The Wasabi warriors broke through the defending ranks a few seconds later, only to meet... nothing. It was as if an entire army had vanished.

As the green and white armies reached the centre of the mountain, they could see a light shining ahead of them; and when they emerged from the tunnel, they found themselves on the other side of the mountain. It was as though the barrier had never existed. And there, on the horizon in front of them, was the outline of the White Queen's besieged castle, silhouetted against the sky.

- Memory Mountain -

Stella and the tribe watched as the phi-flyer landed and the door opened. Aaron, Guido, Ibrahim and the scientist stepped out and looked around, trying to work out where they were. Stella ran across, throwing her arms around her brother's neck. He returned her hug, then held her at arm's length to get a clear look at her.

'You've changed,' he said. 'You look older!'

'You too,' Stella laughed.

'It's time,' Aaron said.

'I know,' Stella said.

'So, introduce me to your new friends.'

Once both of them had introduced everyone, Stella hugged Erika and Josh, then made her way into the phi-flyer. The tribe watched and waved as Marie, Aaron, the scientist, Guido and Ibrahim followed her and the door shut behind them.

Stella and Aaron talked excitedly all the way through the trip, each eager to hear everything that had happened to the other. Before they knew it the phi-flyer had landed and a message popped up on the screen: 'Attention: Memory Mountain.'

The door opened. Outside, they found themselves at the foot of a mountain of unimaginable dimensions. A dark cloud enveloped the distant peak as it soared up into the sky. In front of them was an iron door, and waiting for them beside it was Cassie, his arms spread wide in welcome.

'I'm so glad to see you all,' he said, hugging each of them in turn. 'I will go on with you from here.'

He opened the door and they all filed into a gigantic hall. The walls were covered in racks that stretched all the way up to the roof, with ladders attached so that people could reach the boxes on every shelf, no matter how high.

'What's in all these boxes?' Aaron asked Cassie.

'You are inside the treasure store of the Land of Mushi,' he replied. 'These boxes contain memory bits – the most precious of commodities in the Land of the Mushi.'

'There is untold worth in this room,' Guido said, wide-eyed with excitement.

'We must not touch it,' Aaron warned. 'We haven't earned it.'

They moved cautiously amongst the racks, gazing about them in awe. A sudden clatter made them turn in time to see Guido climbing up one of the ladders.

'Don't touch the bits!' Aaron shouted. 'Or you'll fall under the power of the Black Queen!'

'I've earned this!' Guido yelled back. 'I have been stripped of everything I worked for, and now I have a chance to be rich.'

As he picked up one of the boxes, a group of Wasabi warriors materialised in mid-air. They seized him and then disappeared as quickly as they had appeared, taking Guido with them.

Marie let out a scream of horror, and then began to weep. The others, reeling in shock, tried to calm her, but she was inconsolable.

Aaron put his arm tight around her shaking shoulders. 'When we complete the mission,' he assured her, 'we will find him again. He will have learned his lesson by then.' He had no idea if that was true, but it seemed like the right thing to say.

Marie's barely suppressed sobs, however, dragged all their spirits down as they continued on the mission. They found another iron door and beyond that a staircase, which they climbed nervously, wondering what they would discover at the top. When they finally emerged into the light, they found themselves in the most perfect oasis, standing beneath blossoming trees and beside flowing streams of crystal-clear water. Under the trees were tables laden with sushi energy sources and comfortable seats.

'We can rest and recharge our energy here,' Cassie told them as they flopped gratefully into the soft cushions. He passed around plates of sushi and reviving drinks.

Unable to fight their tiredness any longer, they all drifted into sleep. Aaron found himself in a dream, sailing a boat across calm waters with his father, Igor, and his uncle, Vladimir. Stella dreamed she was swimming in an enormous pool with her mother, Kate, and her aunt, Katya. The dreams were so beautiful and so soothing they both resisted waking up, even though they were aware of Sophie's urgent voice as she danced around the backs of the cushioned chairs, flapping her wings to keep her balance.

'You are in the Zone of Comfort!' she cackled. 'But you will never achieve anything here. You are going to have to force yourselves to take even a single step. You need to leave at once, or you will remain here forever.' Using all the willpower they possessed, Aaron and Stella forced their eyes open and hauled themselves to their feet, spurring the others to follow their example. None of them wanted to move, or even to lift their eyelids, but Aaron and Stella kept pulling at their arms and shouting in their ears until they were all eventually on their feet, blinking like they couldn't work out what was happening.

'We have to go!' Aaron shouted. 'Just follow Cassie.'

Summoning every ounce of energy, the friends set off up a steep mountain path, following it until they came to a cliff face with a line of solid-looking doors carved into its rocks.

'These doors are the passageways to the plateau where the Book is to be found,' Cassie told them. 'But behind half of them there are Zones of Oblivion. I will show you a safe way through.'

He opened one of the doors with a dramatic gesture. 'In here,' he said. 'This is a safe passageway.'

He stood back to allow them all through, then slammed the door behind them, cutting out all light and leaving them falling in a state of complete blackness and emptiness. As they dropped, Cassie's voice echoed in their ears, even though he was already far away on the other side of the door.

'I am Cassie, faithful servant of the Black Queen. It was I who blocked your way through the gorge with stones in the Zone of Intolerance. It was I who drained

the battery of Aaron's Zeno gun in the Zone of Fear. It is I who has guided you into a Zone of Oblivion. Now the game is over, and no one can prevent the Black Queen from achieving absolute victory.'

'What do you have to gain from this betrayal?' Aaron shouted back, as the wind rushed past him.

'Power!' Cassie screamed. 'I can finally seize power from my uncle and become head of the Salmon Mushi – and turn the Cave of Good into a Zone of Evil.'

The sensation of falling through darkness seemed to last forever, but eventually the friends landed and a few shards of grey light reached their eyes from the surrounding oblivion. They stood up and stared at one another. They no longer had any idea who they were, or what had happened in their pasts. All they knew was what they could see and hear and smell at that present moment. Figures in black hoods were busying themselves around the space; one of them beckoned for them to follow him into a corridor, which reeked of sulphur. There seemed no reason not to follow, since they understood nothing of what was going on, and had no memories to help them make decisions for themselves.

The corridor seemed to go on forever before opening out into a grey valley filled with giant wheels, which was where the rotten smell was coming from.

Thousands of people were standing next to the wheels, turning them. Their pale, drained faces were as blank as corpses, their eyes staring blindly from their empty pasts out into an equally empty eternity. The hooded figures led each of the friends to a wheel and instructed them to start turning. There was no reason not to do as they were told.

Back in her besieged castle, the White Queen was studying maps in her throne room when the Lord of Bravery burst in, too agitated even to observe the usual protocol for entering the presence of a queen.

'There has been a disaster, Your Majesty!'

'What has happened?'

'Cassie is a traitor. He has informed the Wasabi warriors about the underground passage. They are now pouring through it into the castle. My soldiers are holding them at bay for the moment, but they are hopelessly outnumbered.'

The Queen straightened her back.
'Well, we have no option other than to fight to the last. Now only the Supreme Ruler can determine our fate.'

Erika was also praying to the Supreme Ruler. Deep inside her thoughts and prayers, a picture began to form as clearly as if it was in front of her eyes – a vision of a grey valley filled with dead-eyed, enslaved people endlessly turning wheels. As the vision grew stronger and more focused she recognised Stella, Aaron and their friends.

She woke from the trance with a clear memory of what she had seen, and in her head she heard Sophie the raven speaking to her: 'When evil reaches its most extreme form, no one can defeat it without the help of the Supreme Ruler.'

Erika closed her eyes. 'O, great Ruler of all,' she prayed. 'You have called upon these people to save our world from the Black Queen, and they have courageously carried out their mission. Please do not leave them in trouble. If, however, your decision is to leave them there, then please send me to the Zone of Oblivion, too.'

When she opened her eyes she saw a phi-flyer in front of her, shining with a magical light. Smiling to herself and sending thanks to the Supreme Ruler, Erika stepped inside and closed the door behind her. The phi-flyer roared forward with a burst of speed, and then appeared to hover above the ground. Erika peered out of the window and saw below the seemingly endless grey valley, full of tiny figures turning giant

wheels, just like in her vision. The bright beam of light from the phi-flyer was penetrating the gloom below like a dawning sun, making many of the toiling figures turn their faces upwards as if to bask in the welcome warmth.

As the light seeped in through their blank eyes, Erika could see flickers of recognition igniting. People began to recognise one another and let go of the wheels as their memories returned and they realised where they were and remembered how they had got there.

After a few minutes the bright light had driven the darkness out completely. Aaron rushed over to Stella and hugged her tightly; the scientist joined them, followed by Ibrahim, Marie, Guido and Miriam.

Eventually they were all laughing and jumping with their arms around one another as the other workers started to walk out of the grim, rocky valley, many with their arms around newly recognised old friends and loved ones from their pasts.

Sophie the raven flapped around in the gradually warming air and called out to Aaron. 'It is time for you to move onward. But beware – the closer you come to the Book, the more strongly the forces of evil will oppose you.'

The friends clambered into the phi-flyer with Erika, surrendering themselves to their fate: they were in the hands of the Supreme Ruler now.

A few minutes later, the phi-flyer landed on a stone plateau. They got out and stared at what lay ahead. Just fifty metres away stood a huge army of Wasabi warriors, just as Sophie had warned. At the front of the terrifying horde stood Datlan and Aliram, and with them was Cassie, transformed now into a fully armed warrior. His easy smile, along with all his other charms, had gone.

Inside the castle of the White Queen, the invading Wasabi were getting closer to the throne room. More and more of the Lord of Bravery's soldiers were overcome by the sheer numbers of their heavily armed attackers, who crushed their fallen bodies underfoot. 'The game is over,' Datlan shouted to the friends on the stone plateau. 'You shall not go any further. Aaron and Stella, listen to me. The Black Queen, in her gracious kindness, has granted permission for you to return to your world. Miriam, you will become my wife, and the rest of you are to be buried in the pit of oblivion.'

Aaron and Stella looked at one another, then down at their red buttons.

'We can't do it,' Stella said. 'We can't leave them.'

'No, we can't,' Aaron agreed. 'But how can we hope to defeat an army this huge and this well-armed, when we have no weapons ourselves?'

'How many times have you appealed to the Supreme Ruler?' Stella asked.

'Once.'

'Me too. That means we can appeal to him one more time.'

As they closed their eyes and sent their appeal deep into the universe, Datlan ran out of patience and ordered his army to advance. The friends could do nothing but watch and wait. As the warriors came closer it was possible to see the murderous blankness on their faces, and just how well-armed they were.

Once they reached the friends, the slaughter would be over in a matter of seconds. There was nowhere to run to and nowhere to hide, and no chance of being able to kill more than a handful of Wasabi before they were overwhelmed. Aaron and Stella both clenched their fists around their red buttons, but held firm and did not press them.

If the attacking army hadn't been making so much noise with their rattling shields and weapons and their rising chants of hatred, they would have heard the buzz from the insect-sized dots that had appeared on the horizon. The friends noticed them first. The dots grew larger, and as they drew close, they could see what they were.

'Phi-flyers!' murmured Aaron.

There were swarms of them. They hummed over the heads of the Wasabi like angry wasps and dropped down onto the stone plateau one after another. The door to the first one opened and Josh burst out at the head of a battalion of his tribal soldiers, all firing neuron pistols as they charged.

Quickly recovering from the surprise, the Wasabi fought back with electrical impulses, sucking their enemies into magnetic traps. The battle was ferocious, but as more soldiers jumped from the phi-flyers, the Wasabi started to falter. Losing confidence, some of them began

to retreat, with Datlan hiding in their midst. Cassie and Aliram fought as ferociously as cornered dogs, but were eventually overwhelmed and taken prisoner.

'I'm going after Datlan!' Josh shouted, ignoring Miriam's pleas not to take any more risks.

Josh caught up with Datlan at the edge of the stone plateau. With a blow fuelled by blazing anger, he brought his former friend crashing to the ground, then jumped on top of him and pushed his arm across his throat. Panic-stricken, Datlan swung a punch at Josh's head, knocking him off balance, then rolled onto him and sank his teeth into Josh's throat. Gasping for breath, Josh brought his knee up hard between Datlan's legs. Datlan screamed, and able to breathe again, Josh grabbed a loose rock and brought it down hard on the back of Datlan's head, sending him toppling to the side. He was out cold. Ripping off Datlan's shirt, Josh used it to tie his arms and legs before he came round.

As he straightened up and looked around, Josh realised that the battlefield had fallen silent. All the Wasabi were either killed or had fled. The friends were standing nearby, exhausted; Stella had her arms around Miriam's shoulders. Josh ran back to them and swept Miriam off her feet, ignoring the blood trickling down his neck from Datlan's teeth marks.

Once they had all hugged each other in relief, they had to decide what to do with their prisoners – Datlan, Aliram and Cassie.

'These people deserve to be imprisoned within a wall of the memory of their betrayal,' Aaron said, after a few moments' thought. 'So that all generations of Mushi will remember and know the names of those who betrayed them.'

Everyone nodded their agreement, and Josh signalled for his soldiers to carry out the sentence. Then suddenly, the plateau was illuminated with a brilliant white light. Aaron, Stella, Guido, Marie, Ibrahim, the scientist and Erika looked up and saw a phi-flyer gently descending from the sky, coming to a rest not three metres away from them. They all shared a glance and jumped straight into it.

Back in her castle, the White Queen was composing herself on her throne, preparing for defeat. From time to time the Lord of Bravery reported to her on the raging battle before dashing back to the fray himself, but the news was never good. She didn't need his reports; she could hear the fighting, and it was getting ever closer to the doors of the throne room. She got herself ready to meet her fate with all the dignity befitting a true queen.

The sounds of the battle intensified yet further. Surely, her time had come. The queen closed her eyes and took several deep breaths. The doors to the throne room exploded open. The White Queen opened her eyes, steeling herself for more bad news.

The Lord of Bravery ran in, covered in wounds from hand-to-hand fighting. But to her amazement, his eyes were wild with a mixture of fury and excitement.

'We are saved!' he shouted. 'Arthur and Salakh's soldiers are here!'

And with that, he ran back out to join the allies. Arthur and Salakh's troops were well-rested, and although the Wasabi struggled fiercely – while at the same time fighting the Lord of Bravery's reinvigorated guards – it wasn't long before they were worn down by exhaustion. Soon, they lay crushed on the flagstones and marble floors of the castle. Not a single one had managed to reach the throne room before the battle was over. They were vanquished.

When the sounds of battle finally died away and peace settled around her, the queen closed her eyes again for a moment and offered personal thanks to the Supreme Ruler.

Then the Lord of Bravery limped back into the throne room. 'Your Majesty,' he said. 'The enemy are defeated. Now we must leave the palace. The six Great White Rulers are waiting for us.'

As the queen looked at the six portals, she saw that they now carried crystal-clear images of the six Great White Rulers.

'Thank you, my Lord,' she said, rising from the throne.

Back in the phi-flyer, Aaron and Stella flew away
from the battle scene, and looked out of the window.

'No!' they screamed in horror.

They were passing so low over a river of fire that the
flames were licking at the underside of the phi-flyer.
It seemed sure that they'd be pulled down into the
red-hot lava. The phi-flyer lurched and for a moment
seemed to lose power; Stella and Aaron clutched
their seats.

The phi-flyer made one enormous effort and rose up,
circling and landing in safety high above the molten lava.
A new message appeared on the screen: 'Attention!
Weapon: quantum measuring device.'

Aaron picked the device up, and they all stepped out.
The phi-flyer had landed on a precipice in front of
a cave; and the odd thing was, its entrance was both
open and closed at the same time.

'This is the Cave of the Book,' Aaron announced,
without being sure how he knew that. 'Let's go in.'

As they moved forward, a cold darkness descended
over them. Fingers of ice swirled on the wind and
grabbed at them, stabbing them, attempting to pull
them off their feet. A single, chilling voice attacked
them from every direction.

'You have overthrown my leaders. You have avoided all the traps I have set. You have destroyed my army. But still, you will never defeat me, the Black Queen, and you will never reach the Book.'

Aaron held up the measuring device with quivering hands and pressed the button, but nothing happened.

'That won't work,' the voice mocked him. 'You can never measure me because there is a part of me in the soul of each of you.'

The voice was drowned out by the louder sound of rushing wind as an ice-cold hurricane roared down on them, carrying them all towards the edge of the precipice as if they weighed no more than feathers.

Stella, the lightest, was swept furthest over the edge.
She clung on by the tips of her fingers as the others
battled to get to her, teetering on the edge of the
abyss themselves. While the cold of the wind burned
them from one side, they could also feel the heat
of the hungry flames that waited far below, ready
to engulf them if they fell. Aaron believed at that
moment that everything was over, and they had lost:
in the next few moments they would all be burned
and gone.

But then Sophie the raven appeared above them. She too was being buffeted by the winds, but was skilfully using their currents so that they couldn't dash her against the cliff face.

'Throw the measuring device to Ibrahim!' she screamed to Aaron above the roar of the wind. 'Even the Black Queen has no power over a sinner who has said he's sorry.'

Aaron flung the device, and Ibrahim managed to grab it before it plummeted out of sight over the precipice. He pressed the button and the wind was instantly stilled. The fog cleared and sunlight broke through again.

As the White Queen emerged from her castle with the Lord of Bravery, Arthur and Salakh, Albert followed behind at a respectful distance. Before them stood the six Great White Rulers, and behind them a jubilant crowd of cheering Mushi.

The White Queen held up her hand for silence. 'The Black Queen has been defeated and will never return,' she told the crowd. 'Remember this, and may this day every year be a holiday when the Mushi celebrate and rejoice in their miraculous deliverance.'

Back at the precipice, Aaron pulled his sister up onto the path and they walked together to the entrance of the cave. Aaron stretched his arm out and for a few minutes nothing happened. He did not lower his arm, just kept staring ahead with a look of deep concentration and certainty. His sister squeezed his other hand in encouragement, but said nothing.

They both closed their eyes tightly shut, willing the door to open with every ounce of energy they could muster.

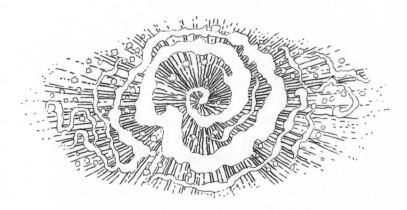

- Epilogue -

When Aaron and Stella eventually opened their eyes they found themselves waking up back in the restaurant, entwined on the bench seat.

They looked at one another in horror. How could this be? How could the adventure be over without them ever knowing whether the door had opened and whether they had succeeded in returning the Book to the people? Everyone around them was laughing and talking, but they just wanted to be able to close their eyes and get back to the precipice.

'Welcome back, you two,' their grandfather laughed. 'You've been asleep for at least an hour.'

'You must have worn yourselves out in the sea,' their grandmother said.

'Or stuffed yourselves with too much sushi,' their grandfather added.

'You've missed ice creams,' their younger sister Erika told them, with a look of supreme pleasure on her sticky little face.

'We didn't want to wake you,' their Aunt Sophie said. 'You looked so peaceful, like you didn't have a care in the world.'

As the family gathered themselves together to leave the restaurant, Mr Ekaku went to open the door for them, bowing respectfully as they thanked him for the meal. Aaron gazed wonderingly at him, and Mr Ekaku caught his eye, ever so briefly. He could have sworn that he saw the waiter wink.

'How was the special sushi, Mr Aaron and Miss Stella?' he asked.

'It was epic, thank you, Mr Ekaku,' Aaron said, politely returning his bow.

'I don't believe I will ever forget it,' Stella added, mirroring her brother's low bow.

'Everyone is very grateful to you for coming,' Mr Ekaku said, pressing a delicate piece of folded paper into Stella's hand discreetly. She held onto it tightly as the family began to stroll off into the cool evening air.

Then she tugged at her brother's arm. 'Aaron,' she whispered. 'He's given me a message.'

They dropped back behind the rest of the family and as soon as it was safe, Stella unfolded the paper. It released a golden glow which lit up their faces as they read the message inscribed inside.

As they watched, the corners of the paper began to curl up as if caught in the flames of an invisible fire. A few seconds later there was nothing but dust lying in Stella's outstretched palm.

Aaron and Stella looked at each other and smiled.

First published in 2019 by White Raven Publishing

ISBN 978-1-912892-15-0
Also available as an ebook
ISBN 978-1-912892-30-3

Book design by Strawberrie Donnelly
Project management by whitefox
Printed and bound by Ozgraf, Poland